HER ENEMY PROTECTOR

TEMPT ME SERIES

AVERY FLYNN

Entangled Publishing, LLC
2614 South Timberline Road
Suite 109
Fort Collins, CO 80525
Visit our website at www.entangledpublishing.com.

Indulgence is an imprint of Entangled Publishing, LLC.

Edited by Alethea Spiridon
Cover design by Bree Archer
Cover art from Shutterstock

Manufactured in the United States of America

First Edition November 2016

Chapter One

Blackmail was first up on the agenda today. It wasn't nice, but then again, neither was he.

Major Lucas Bendtsen got out of his BMW Roadster parked in front of the three-story manor house and surveyed his new home that went along with his recently bestowed title, Earl of Moad. The manor house stood on a fjord overlooking the North Sea; the water crashed against the rocks. Five hundred miles to the east lay Norway. Roughly four hundred miles to the south was Scotland. In between it was just the deep blue ocean.

It wasn't the bright lights of Harbor City on the American East Coast or the constant crush of people in London, but he could get used to it. After growing up on the streets of Elskov's capital and doing whatever it took to survive, he'd learned the hard way that he could get used to anything and rise above it. The millions in his bank account proved that.

A gentleman spymaster, that's what the addict's son who'd grown into a criminal had become, with a country house and a title. An aristocrat. His mother would have died of surprise if the needle hadn't gotten to her already. His father? Well, if he knew who the fuck that bastard had been, maybe then he'd worry about his reaction.

His phone vibrated in his suit pocket, a reminder that while he might be lord of the manor, he was also the secret head of the Silver Knights, an elite intelligence and fighting arm answerable only to the Queen of Elskov herself.

He took out his cell and glanced at the caller ID. Agent Talia Clausen headed up Operation Family Jewels. Whoever had picked that name deserved a kick in his.

Lucas pressed the talk button. "Yes?"

"Sir, we have her. She's on her way to you now."

Adrenaline spiked in his system, and he began pacing in front of the manor house. "Does she know why?"

"Negative. She thinks you are interested in having her design a jeweled family crest befitting your new station in life."

God. That made him sound like a total knob. People actually did that? He shook his head. "And the brother?"

"In custody."

"Good. Don't let him go." The scumbag deserved a nice long stay behind bars for bringing two kilos of cocaine into Elskov, but the asshole was still useful, so instead of jail he was sitting in comfort in a safe house on the isolated south shore. "He's our best leverage to get her to do what we need."

"Are you sure this is the best plan? There are risks."

Lucas stopped in his tracks. This wasn't the best plan—it was the only plan. They had one shot, and he wasn't about to let the sexy little jewelry designer, Ruby Macintosh, get away without agreeing to his terms. The number of men who ended up the victims of jewel theft, murdered during a robbery, or never heard from again after tangling with the mobster's stepdaughter was in dispute, but fifty was probably in the conservative range. The only question was, did the bombshell lure the men into her stepfather's web or do the dirty deeds herself?

Not that it mattered. He'd use her to protect Elskov from attack by the tattered remains of the Fjende. With their leader, Walther Henriksen, dead, most of the men behind the coup that had taken over the country for the past decade had scattered and disavowed their treasonous acts, but not everyone.

"You've read the same reports as I have," he said, not bothering to keep the icy clip out of his voice. "Walther Henriksen's son, Gregers, came out of hiding just long enough to put the word out that he wants to buy enough weaponry from the Macintosh organization to take over a small country. Three guesses about which country that is. Blackmailing Ruby Macintosh is the fastest way to stop an attack before it happens."

"Just be sure you don't fall under her spell. She has a reputation."

"So do I." He grinned. If the woman on the other end of the phone could have seen it, she would have taken three steps back. "Be at my office at six tomorrow morning for a briefing. This operation is a go."

Lucas hung up the phone and turned toward the mile-long driveway. Ruby Macintosh would arrive within minutes, and then, one way or another, her life would change forever. He'd see to it.

· · ·

Where in the hell was her brother?

Driving through the Earl of Moad's guarded gate, Ruby Macintosh followed the winding driveway through what seemed like a million miles of perfectly manicured lawn dotted by the occasional massive, old yew tree as the never-answered ringing of her brother's cell phone trilled through her Peugeot RCZ Sport Coupe's speakers. The sound drilled right down her spine, partnering up with the worry eating away at her stomach lining to make her see red. He always did this. *Always.* One of these days he was going to pay for all the shit he pulled trying to get on their stepfather's good side, even she'd figured out by the ripe old age of eleven that the old man had nothing but a bad side.

"You know the drill," her brother's voice came over the speaker. "Here comes the beep."

Her grip tightened on the steering wheel as she followed the bend in the driveway, and the pale yellow manor house appeared ahead. "Jasper, you better hope I find you before Rolf does. He's got the Sparrow ready to mobilize. I can't cover for your scrawny ass—*again*—unless I know what I'm up against. Call me."

She punched end call on the car's Bluetooth.

Her best friend, Ilsa Jakobsen, kept asking why she had no interest in settling down with Mr. Right and popping out some kids. She had two very good reasons that Ilsa knew already. One, Jasper was enough of a responsibility. Two, her darling stepfather had a literal trigger finger when it came to anyone who might pull her even a tad bit further away from his control—especially when he had Joey Brotzka waiting in the wings with a tacky-ass engagement ring in his pocket, which is exactly where it was going to stay—no matter how much bitching Rolf did.

That was a catastrophe for another day, though. Right now she had to meet her newest design client and then fix Jasper's latest disaster.

Easing her lead foot off the gas pedal—what a sad thing to have to do—she went over an honest-to-God moat that crossed in front of the large three-story house and came to a stop outside of the manor's double doors. There was a BMW parked off to the side but not a single other sign of human inhabitance. The whole estate had an overly-structured, demanding, and hard beauty to it. It wasn't unwelcoming, but she couldn't shake the feeling of being judged and found lacking.

Ruby parked and grabbed her kit from the passenger seat then got out of the car. Even though it was spring, there was still enough of a chill in the air to make her thankful for her favorite black moto jacket. Out of habit more than need, she locked her car before heading for the steps leading to the front door.

It opened before she had her foot on the first step. A man stood in the doorway wearing jet-black suit pants and a white shirt undone at the collar with the sleeves rolled halfway up his sinewy forearms. Dark hair, aquamarine eyes, and a five o'clock shadow that only emphasized the sensual curve of his lips finished off the package. Making sure to keep her jaw from hitting the floor, she thanked the fates for giving her a little bit of eye candy to go along with what was sure to be a pain in the ass job.

In her experience, the aristocratic types in high-maintenance homes rarely knew what they wanted in their one-of-a-kind jewelry and jewel designs but sure as hell knew what they didn't want, which translated to days wasted on about a thousand design proposal sketches that would be turned down.

"Ms. Macintosh, I'm Lucas Bendtsen" he said smoothly. "Thank you for coming."

"But of course," she said slipping into the soft consonants and rounded vowels of her upper-crust clients. She'd found out early that speaking in her normal hard-edged, non-Elskovian accent didn't exactly give them confidence in her taste level as a jewelry designer. "I'm excited to be a part of this project, sir."

"Please, call me Lucas." He held open the door for her. "I have tea set up in the sitting room."

"Lovely." After spending all night searching Jasper's favorite Faroe City haunts she could really go for an espresso or twelve, but tea would have to do.

She glanced up—way, way up—at him as she walked inside. He had to have more than a foot on her five feet two inches. Not for the first time in her life she wished she had that tall, willowy thing all of the Elskovian girls that she'd gone to boarding school with had. Instead, she had football player shoulders and an ass that could not be contained—not that she didn't love that last bit, even though it did make shopping for jeans a nightmare.

Crossing the threshold, she passed into a large foyer dominated by a circular marble table. Two men stood on either side of a door off to the right. Hands clasped in front of them, nondescript suits, and with their faces wearing matching blank expressions, there was no missing that they were muscle.

Apprehension snaked it way up her spine, leaving a trail of goose bumps in its wake. She'd grown up at the knee of a master when it came to subterfuge and double-dealing. Had it made her paranoid, or should she be regretting that she'd left her Beretta in the car's glove box?

Normally, she would have done her homework on the new earl, but with the last minute request by his assistant and the late-night search for Jasper, she hadn't. That was a mistake she'd correct as soon as she got back to her tiny apartment in Faroe City. Still, she suppressed her Nervous Nita reaction. The earl's assistant had come with a reference from one of her best clients when she'd booked the appointment. With her history, who was she to judge someone else's quirks?

He strode over to the door between the guards, his long, lean legs closing the distance in only a few strides. "Right this way."

She squared her shoulders and followed him into a room that took her breath away. One wall was made up entirely of windows that overlooked the manor house's formal French-style garden. Boxwood hedges, elaborately shaped shrubs, and precisely planted garden beds lined stone paths that lead to a large fountain. Beyond it was a gorgeous expanse of lavender, made even more heavenly by the appearance of several teak lounge chairs where a person could sit, read, and inhale the scent in the spring sunshine.

"It's beautiful." She sighed.

The dark lines of his eyebrows squished together. "What is?"

She nodded toward the windows. "The garden."

He looked out the window for a moment before shrugging his shoulders. "I hadn't really noticed." He sat down on one of the small couches that faced each other on opposite sides of the richly colored tapestry rug.

Okay then. She was going to work on a design with a possibly blind, paranoid rich guy who just happened to be super hot. This was going to be awesome. She took out her portfolio from the large canary yellow bag that housed everything she needed in her traveling design kit and sat down at the other end of the couch from the earl. It was as far away as she could get from him and still be able to show him her portfolio, but it was too close. There was something unsettling about the way he was looking at her with those blue-green eyes, like he very much enjoyed the view even though he didn't want to. Men liked her. She liked them. That was never a problem…unless her stepfather found out and decided they could be used for his own gain.

She flipped the portfolio open and handed it to him. "I've brought several examples of other Elskovian family crests and some initial ideas for the new Earl of Moad crest."

He didn't look down at the intricate drawing of a jeweled swan sitting atop a golden crown. "That won't be necessary."

There it was again. That sliver of worry mixed with an excited anticipation dancing across her skin. "You already have something in mind?"

"No." He dropped her portfolio onto the coffee table, barely missing the pristine tea service. "I have no interest in getting a crest made. What I want is the unlimited access to your stepfather and his criminal empire that only you can give me—and you will because you don't have a choice. Until the operation is finished, you are mine."

• • •

He watched her wide-eyed gaze flicker to the door before snapping back to him, fury simmering in their gray depths.

"I wouldn't recommend it. Gustav and Mads aren't known for slacking on the job." He paused. "And I promise you, Ms. Macintosh, neither am I."

Despite knowing he shouldn't like anything about her, he couldn't help but admire the way she schooled her features into a look of superior disdain. God, he loved a challenge.

Instead of yelling or crying or making a mad dash for it, like so many others would have, her lips curled in an icy facsimile of a smile, and she reached for the delicate porcelain teapot on the coffee table. Like every other household item here, it had come with the manor.

As she filled one of the tiny cups with tea, he took the opportunity to better size her up. She was not what he expected. Creative types were always a little bit…different, but she was a study in contradictions. She'd kept her natural honey-wheat colored hair, but it was streaked with thick swaths of pink, blue, and purple. The prim and proper white dress she wore managed to hug her every sinful curve but was set off with a worn leather jacket and the hint of a tattoo starting on her wrist and disappearing up her sleeve. Then there was her face, with its almost innocent beauty punctuated with glossy, hot-pink lips that would give a priest dirty thoughts.

"Do you take sugar?" she asked, interrupting his perusal and giving him a knowing look.

Blood rushed to his cock in anticipation. "No."

"Too bad." She handed him the cup on a saucer, brushing her finger across his in the process and making his skin tingle. "I think you could use some sweetness in your life."

Obviously she was toying with him, playing the games that had always netted her a prize before. No woman—no matter how tempting—would ever tug his attention away from his ultimate goal. Elskov's safety hung in the balance. Lucas wouldn't be responsible for the chaos that would ensue if Gregers Henriksen got his hands on enough weapons to start an ugly, guerrilla-style war.

Sitting back and crossing one ankle across his knee, he kept his face neutral. "Are you lecturing me or trying to taunt me into changing my mind?"

"Neither," she said. "I was making an observation."

He took a sip of tea, which did taste more bitter than usual—a fact that only annoyed him more. "Well, you can keep them to yourself during this operation."

"That will be easy." Her posture perfect and her chin tipped upward at the exact angle to deliver a nonverbal "fuck you," Ruby took a drink. "I'm going to finish my tea and then walk out of this house forever. I won't be a part of whatever it is you have planned."

"Yes, you will." He set his cup and saucer down and picked up the black folder next to the tea service. "If you don't, your brother is going to spend the rest of his life rotting in jail."

Her hand shook as she put her teacup down and took the folder from him. This time there wasn't any accidentally-on-purpose touching or coy looks from under her thick lashes.

The first page was taken up almost completely by Jasper Macintosh's mug shot. He'd had another agent enlarge the photo so Ruby would be sure to see every millimeter of the dark circles under her little brother's eyes and the worry lurking behind the bravado. Her jaw tightened, and she swallowed hard but didn't say anything before flipping to the next page. Much of it was blacked out because the case was ongoing, but she would be able to read the basic facts. Jasper had been caught with two kilos of cocaine in the trunk of his rented Ferrari after police received an anonymous tip. Had someone set him up? No doubt. Lucas didn't care if the caller had been a disgruntled Macintosh crew member or someone from a rival gang. All he cared about was that the arrest gave him the leverage he needed.

After a few minutes, she closed the folder and tossed it onto the coffee table. It landed half on top of her abandoned cup of tea but managed not to knock it over.

"Who are you really?" she asked, anger making her shed the formal accent she'd put on earlier. The hard-edged, lightly accented alto fit her better than the fake upper-crust thing she was using before.

"Exactly who you think." He lied as easily as he breathed, a skill learned by necessity at too young an age. "Lucas Bendtsen, the newest Earl of Moad."

She arched one eyebrow. "The rest of it now."

Challenge made the tiny green flecks in her gray eyes brighten. She had some serious spirit, this one, and an excellent bullshit detector. Considering with whom she'd grown up, that wasn't a surprise. Still, he was a little too pleased by the discovery.

"I'm head of Silver Knights."

She flinched. It was small, imperceptible to most, but he'd seen the flash of apprehension at the name of Elskov's version of the CIA, FBI, MI6, and Interpol all mixed together into one badass operation with only one goal: to protect Elskov and its queen, who'd been recently restored to the throne after a bloody coup that had nearly destroyed the country.

"Good to see you know of our reputation and now realize the seriousness of your situation—and that of your brother."

Her cheeks flushed. "You're a right bastard."

"Literally and figuratively. I've learned to live with it, so should you," he said, glad to finally have the upper hand. Usually, that wasn't a problem. With Ruby? He had a feeling he was going to have to expect the unexpected. "We're under a tight deadline and don't have time for petty personality problems. Your stepfather is selling a large cache of weapons to a very bad man who wants to do horrible things. I will not let that sale go down, and you're going to do whatever it takes to help me ensure it doesn't."

He wasn't about to give her names—not until he had to—but she had to comprehend the seriousness of the situation.

She huffed out a frustrated breath. "And how am *I* supposed to do that?"

So glad she asked. It was about time they got down to it. "By providing access to your stepfather and helping to gain insight into the deal's location."

"One problem with your plan," she said with a smirk. "I'm not involved in any of Rolf's business. For the past year I've kept as much distance between us as possible. You'll notice I'm here in Elskov, and he's still holed up in his private fiefdom on Fare Island, surrounded by goons and sycophants."

Oh he knew. He had satellite imagery of everything happening on that island. If Henriksen ever came anywhere near that island, he'd find his every twitch photographed, logged, and documented before he ended up in maximum security prison.

"Not to worry," he said. "We have a plan. It's time for a

family reunion."

She blanched. "You don't understand. He trusts no one. Not me. Not Jasper. Not anyone."

That didn't matter; in fact, they were going to use that to their advantage. "We have a can't-miss cover story."

"I'm telling you," she said, her low, sultry voice getting louder with each word. "There's. No. Way. It. Will. Work."

"There's always a way." If he didn't believe that, then he'd still be living in a rented room above the Ensom Pub surviving on his wits and the scraps of information he could steal and sell to the highest bidder. Instead, here he was the literal lord of the manor charged with protecting Elskov. "There's always a way, and if there's not, I make one."

She considered him for a moment, her gray eyes focused on him as if he were a safe she was cracking, then she sighed and shrugged her shoulders. "I don't suppose I have a choice."

"No, you don't."

"Then it looks like we have a deal." She held out her hand.

He took it, shaking on the agreement. The feel of her small hand in his sent a jolt straight from his palm to his already half-hard dick. He couldn't deny the woman's sex appeal, but he couldn't fall prey to it, either. The men who had were either broke, in jail, or dead. He'd managed to successfully avoid all three up to now and that wasn't going to change.

"Of course," she said, pulling her hand from his and looking down at her own hand in half wonder and half concern, as if she'd experienced that zap of attraction, too. "I do have two conditions."

He almost laughed. She didn't give up, a quality he couldn't help but admire even if it meant she was going to be a real pain in his ass. "And those are?"

"One, you get Jasper out of jail and into protective custody." She looked him dead in the eye without a flinch, her neutral poker face in perfect order. "My stepfather has many enemies, and while he may not trust my brother, he would see any harm done to Jasper as a personal affront. His enemies would be thrilled to exploit that vulnerability."

Not a problem since they already had him squirreled away under twenty-four-hour guard with two of his most trusted agents. "Done. And the other?"

"Give me the space I need to get whatever information you need." She held up a finger. "No wires." She held up a second. "No cameras. I'll bring you back the information you want, but I have to do it in my own way."

"No." Not even if hell froze over.

Her hand dropped like a lead weight into her lap. "No?"

"No." He leaned forward, close enough that he could smell her exotic perfume and see the way the vein in her neck stood out as her pulse picked up from his nearness. "You see, *I'm* your cover story and the reason for your return trip to Fare Island. We're officially engaged and about to invite your mother and stepfather to our wedding. As long as those weapons are out there, Ms. Macintosh, there won't be any daylight between us."

Chapter Two

She was in a puffy, pink nightmare.

Ruby looked around the guest room she'd been assigned, aka Barbie's LSD nightmare. From the sheer blush of the walls to the Pepto-Bismol duvet cover on the bed, there was pink everywhere she looked. It was like karma coming back to haunt her for insisting on getting the magenta highlights along with the violet ones, despite Isla warning her she might want to dial it down a notch — or twenty.

She sat her heavy design travel kit down on the taffy-colored rug and did a three-sixty. Although they'd been colored to match the overbearing design scheme, she picked out two motion detectors, a trigger alarm on the door, and sensors around the windows. There was probably more, but she didn't have the stomach to find out if the bathroom was done up in shades of watermelon or salmon, so checking in there would have to wait. Just the idea of a fifty-shades-of-pink bathroom made the designer in her throw up a little. Still, there had to be a way out of this room, and she'd find it. Lucas may think he had a winning scheme to get those guns, but she knew better.

Rolf Macintosh hadn't become the most dangerous and successful gunrunner and profiteer in Northern Europe by being stupid. He'd taken over crime syndicates, banished rivals, and decimated his opposition by being willing to do what others wouldn't and never trusting another living soul.

Not his wife.

Not his adopted stepchildren.

No one.

She had to find a way out of this pink prison and rescue her brother. Then they'd find a way to disappear for good. If she didn't, they were both as good as dead.

Crossing to the door, she considered her options. She was up on the third floor, too far for a window ladder made out of sheets to work—even if the windows weren't rigged. She turned the doorknob and peeked out. The testosterone twins from outside the sitting room had moved upstairs to take up position outside her door.

"Did you need something, ma'am?" one of them asked.

Mads? Gustav? No fucking clue.

"Where's Lucas?" she asked.

"Major Bendtsen, I mean the earl, is in his study," the first twin responded.

"Thank you." Every tidbit of information had the potential to be useful.

Twin Two glared in her direction and crossed his massive arms across his expansive chest.

Yeah, I got it. Big, bad, bulky men stop weak, little woman. How her eyes managed to stay in her head after the massive eye roll she executed would remain a mystery.

She closed the door as she ran the manor's layout through her head like a film reel. They'd passed the room that had to be Lucas's study when he'd marched her up to her temporary puke-pink prison. She'd peeked through the door as he'd had a hushed discussion with another agent. A huge fireplace was at one end of the room and a pin-neat desk at the other. It was all mahogany, leather, and brass—not even a whisper of softness in the entire room.

The guard's slip up about Lucas's title was telling. Either her blackmailer was new to the aristocracy, or he was lying to her. She paced to the window and back again, over and over, considering the question and its implications.

Who exactly was Lucas Bendtsen?

Was he a major in the Elskov military?

Was he the Earl of Moad?

Was he head of the Silver Knights?

She had no proof of either identity or proof that he wasn't someone else entirely.

The longer she considered the unanswered questions, the more her stomach roiled as her apprehension built. Then it hit her, stopping her in her tracks right in front of her powder-puff-colored door. A slimy, toxic dread slithered through her.

It would be just like him.

Her stepfather loved his games—the more elaborate, the better. If he'd decided to test her loyalty, test the promise she'd made before she'd finally escaped Fare Island, this was how he'd do it. He'd set her up, fuck with her head, and see if she broke so he could finally do what he'd always threatened and force her to marry Joey. For years she'd lived in fear of his evil plots, but those days were over. Powered by righteous indignation and adrenaline, she flung the door open and marched out into the hall.

"Ma'am," one of the twins said. "You're not supposed to go anywhere."

She spun around to face him, the contempt on her face daring him to do something about it. He wouldn't. Her stepfather always liked to dole out the punishments himself.

"Are you going to shoot me?"

Twin One opened his mouth, but nothing came out. Exactly what she expected. "Then stay the fuck out of my way."

She stormed down the stairs to the main floor and made a beeline for Lucas's study. The door was closed. She twisted the knob. Locked. Eyeballing the doorknob as she fished around in her pocket for one of the spare bobby pins she kept there out of habit, she grinned and gave the lock a second look. She could have popped it when she was eight.

Ten seconds later, she flung open the door and stalked inside Lucas's private domain. "I don't know who you are, you son of a—"

The last word died on her lips as she stood facing Elskov's beautiful, twenty-something queen, or at least a huge image of her projected onto the video screen above the fireplace. She wasn't wearing a tiara or anything, but there was no mistaking the woman who'd survived an attempted assassination and married a hunk of a man who, rumor had it, kidnapped her to save her from the men who would have gladly killed her.

"Oh, I see you're making friends, Lucas. I knew you had it in you," the queen said in her half-Elskovian, half-American accent. "You've completely confirmed my decision to make you head of the Silver Knights."

Out of her peripheral vision, Ruby spotted Lucas glowering at her in that whole dangerous badass way he had, which, it turned out, he'd totally earned. She pressed one clammy palm to her stomach.

The Silver Knights were a thing of legend in Elskov. No one knew exactly who was in the Silver Knights and especially not who lead them. They'd taken down terrorists, well-connected assassins, and anyone else threatening Elskov. Even her father, a despotic braggart, talked about them in hushed tones. The Silver Knights were the boogeymen to anyone in Northern Europe's criminal underworld who gave even a hint that they might disturb the kingdom's peace.

"Don't let that nasty look on Lucas's face fool you. He's only two-thirds asshole. I promise," the queen said. "You must be the infamous Ruby Macintosh I've heard so much about."

She dropped into a jittery, poor excuse of a curtsey. "Yes, Your Majesty."

"Please do get up. I'm an Americanized Elskovian, I just can't get used to all of that."

"You're not supposed to say that." A muscular, blond man strode into view. There was no mistaking Dominick Rasmussen, Elskov's king. "What will our little prince say?"

"That Daddy has a big mouth." The queen grinned, obviously too ecstatically happy to put any heat in the insult.

"It's just Bendtsen." He looked away from the queen for the first time since appearing on screen. His gaze locked with hers and in a split second he went from the doting husband to a man well used to people always following his orders. "And...someone who is sworn to secrecy or we open up the castle's dungeons again."

"Stop teasing her." The queen rolled her eyes. "We're trying to get her on our side."

Ruby straightened and kept her attention focused on the queen and her king even as she felt Lucas prowl closer to her, setting off her fight-or-flight response.

The queen smiled. "Lucas tells me you're hesitant about our plan."

Her ultimate plan had been to somehow grab Jasper and run, but discovering exactly who she was up against meant escape wasn't an option—at least not now. Not that she was going to go all sweet and agreeable on her blackmailer.

Squaring her shoulders, she tucked her hair behind one ear, raised her chin, and looked the queen straight in the eye. "I don't think it will work."

"It is risky, I agree." The queen nodded. "However, Lucas

has quite convinced me, otherwise I wouldn't have authorized such...extreme measures."

"That's what you call this?" she asked, frustration making her voice shake.

Lucas moved closer to her, the dark, censorious look on his face warning her against any more outbursts. It took everything she had not to signal her response with a one-fingered salute.

"Don't worry, he's helped kidnap me before, too," the queen said with a light chuckle. "That ended up working out well for everyone involved. I know it doesn't seem like it, but you can trust Lucas and his plan. It will work. I wouldn't trust the fate of Elskov to just anyone. I know he'll do whatever it takes to keep the country safe. On behalf of all Elskovians, please accept my gratitude for agreeing to play a part in this operation—not that I had any doubt in Lucas's ability to get you to see the light."

Ruby slid her gaze over to the man in question. He was holding the black folder he'd shown her earlier with Jasper's arrest report in it. The taste of rotten milk coated her tongue as dread wound around her throat. The message couldn't be clearer: cooperate or Jasper pays the price. Knowing exactly who Lucas was, she didn't have a single doubt that he'd follow through with his threat. For the first time in her life, she wished it had been her stepfather playing his sick head games.

"Now," the queen continued, "if we don't have anything else, Lucas?"

"No, Your Majesty," he said.

"I'd wish you good luck, but you won't need it. We'll talk again soon." The image on the video screen swapped from the queen and king to the Elskovian State Seal.

Mind whirling around the ever shrinking possibilities of getting out of this situation alive and with the odds running even on whether her stepfather or Lucas would finish off her and Jasper first, she turned toward the door. The need to get out of here before the walls closed in on her had her so focused on escape, she missed Lucas's quick movements until he stood between her and the open doorway.

Never taking his attention off her, Lucas closed the door behind him. His spacious study suddenly shrank in size, and her pulse quickened. He didn't say anything—he just stared with those all-knowing blue-green eyes that unsettled her.

Desire heated her skin as if there was a blaze burning in the huge fireplace across the room. It made her lungs tight and her breasts heavy as warmth pooled low in her stomach. Her reaction to being close to him had to be a side effect from running on adrenaline since she'd realized Jasper was missing last night. Or maybe it was because she'd gotten a little too used to boyfriends who were battery powered. It wasn't—couldn't be—because of him. She wouldn't let it.

His gaze dropped to her mouth and then to the peaked tips of her nipples pressing against the white knit jersey of her dress, the thin material disguising nothing. Embarrassed at her body's obvious response to him that she couldn't hide, she brushed past him and reached for the door.

His hand covered hers on the doorknob before she even had a chance to twist her wrist to open the door. Looking back over her shoulder, she noted he stood directly behind her with only a few inches separating their bodies.

"The queen is right, you know," he said, his warm breath brushing against the exposed column of her neck and setting off a shiver of lust. "I will do whatever it takes and make any sacrifices necessary to safeguard my country. Consider that before you try anything that might sabotage this operation." He paused as her heart hammered against her ribs. "The queen is also wrong. I'm a *complete* asshole used to *always* having my way. You'd better remember that before you go bursting into any more rooms without an invitation."

Blood rushing in her ears and desire slowing her thinking, it took a second to realize that he'd released her hand and stepped away. Once she did, her survival instinct kicked in, and she flew out the door, hurrying up the staircase to her room where she could regroup and come up with a plan not to sabotage herself by falling into bed with her blackmailer.

Chapter Three

Rainbow on the move.

Sitting at the dining room table, Lucas read the text message from Gustav and then glanced back down at the schematics of Rolf Macintosh's stronghold disguised as a sprawling country house spread out before him. Though he looked at the architectural plan, he couldn't help but picture the rainbow-haired woman who'd stormed into his office spitting mad this afternoon.

His cock stirred at the memory of being so close to her that he'd nearly given in to the temptation of nibbling a path up the narrow column of her neck. The way her nipples had tented under the thin material of her dress as he'd leaned in close to warn her not to do anything stupid had almost pushed him over the edge. Of course, that was exactly the reaction she'd been going for. It was the one men always seemed to have around her, and one she used to her advantage, according to her file.

Not that his cock was listening to the warnings his brain was sending out.

If he didn't watch it, Lucas would become one more chump on the long list of sad saps who'd fallen for Ruby's femme fatale charms. He couldn't—wouldn't—let that happen.

The sound of high heels on the marble floor drifted in from the hall outside the dining room's open double doors. Rolling up the blueprints, he settled his features into a neutral mask that gave away nothing and rounded the long, formal table to the end where two place settings had been arranged around a trio of beeswax candles. Obviously, someone on staff thought they had a sense of humor—too bad he didn't. First Operation Family Jewels and now an ironic romantic setting. He was going to have to have a talk with the team. He wet his fingers and pinched out the candles' flames.

"Are we celebrating our engagement with a romantic dinner?" Ruby asked from the doorway, one hand on her hip and a smirk curling her full, pink lips.

Mads must have returned from a necessary trip to her apartment because she'd changed. Gone was the virginal white dress. Now she wore a loose white shirt casually tucked into the narrow waist of a pair of strategically ripped jeans. A bright cluster of necklaces crossed the deep V neckline of her shirt, coming to rest in the deep valley between her tits. By the time his gaze made it up from her black heels to her face, she'd paired her knowing grin with an arched eyebrow for an overall smug, caught-you-peeking look.

If he were the type to get embarrassed, he would be. However, he'd given up that useless emotion years ago, along with anything else that could get in the way of him accomplishing his goals.

"More of a working dinner," he said, pulling out his chair and sitting down.

Following his lead, she sat down next to him. "And what is on the agenda?" she asked, her tart tone betraying the blasé expression she wore like a shield.

"Your life story." He needed to find out the things she may not think mattered that could make the difference in whether or not Rolf Macintosh fell for the ruse or saw right through to the truth.

Her expression hardened, irritation flashing in her gray eyes. "I figured you already had a black folder filled with all of my secrets already."

"Most of them."

Three inches thick and detailed, his file on her held every piece of fact, rumor, and innuendo his team had dug up on her. But he needed more. As much as he discounted any kind of emotion, it was the key to creating a believable cover.

"Is this really necessary?" She sawed off a hunk of pork covered in a creamy parsley sauce, wielding the knife with more force than required.

"This operation hinges on your stepfather believing we're an actual couple about to be married so that I can gain access to his base of operations and uncover the time and date of the arms deal." He sliced off a bite of pork with precision. "If we can't manage that, then we're both in deep shit."

"I suppose that means you'll be spilling your guts to me?"

He almost choked, revulsion sticking in his throat at the idea. "No. I've used a certain cover for years now. It's established and without even a hint of illegitimacy—at least of the kind that would make your father pause." He nodded toward the black folder next to her salad fork. "Everything you need to know is in there. You have tonight to memorize it. We leave in the morning."

She picked up the thick folder and flipped through it. "A little light reading, huh?"

"If you expected life to be easy, you should have stayed at Fare Island."

"Is that what you think my life was like with my dear old stepdad? Easy?" She snorted and shook her head.

"Are you trying to tell me that living life in the lap of luxury surrounded by celebrities, servants, and guards wasn't?"

He knew all about the Macintosh fiefdom on Fare Island. Models, the Hollywood elite, and world leaders of questionable morals coveted invitations there to indulge in all the illicit offerings the most notorious crime boss in Europe could offer. In exchange, he and his family wallowed in luxury goods from the chocolates their maids left on their pillows as if they lived in a hotel to the designer clothes Ruby wore tonight. She'd never had her stomach so empty it practically folded in on itself or learned the power of a solid, hard punch when the other kid in foster care had a good twenty pounds and three years on you.

"Do you know who the Sparrow is?" She laid her fork and knife down in an X across her half-eaten dinner with a hard clank.

"Of course." Thin and wiry with a beak of a nose and a disturbing, nearly unblinking stare, Hamish Hansen had come by his nickname honestly.

"Let me tell you what you may not know about the most feared knife in Europe. He didn't just lay down the law with anyone who crossed my stepfather, but with Jasper and me too." She flipped her left hand over and shoved her palm toward him. "This was my punishment after I took one of my father's sailboats in an attempt to get to Elskov."

The scar had faded to pale white lines that formed a fancy capital *M* and *I* with decorative swoops and bends. According to the rumors in her file, she'd carved it herself as a show of loyalty and commitment to the family business.

"It took him less than five minutes to fillet my palm." She flexed her hand and curled her fingers into a fist a few times, watching the carved-in brand appear and disappear without even a flicker of rage or hurt or fear appearing on her face. "Really, you have to admire his craftsmanship. He inflicted just enough damage to serve as a reminder of what happens to anyone who steals from Rolf Macintosh but managed not to maim me. I think he figured he was doing me a favor. He was, after all, the one who gave me my first sketch pad."

His head said she was lying, but his gut said something else. There was just enough...nothingness in her calm voice and unlined face to give her—and the truth—away.

"And your father accepted this?" he asked, working hard to keep his tone neutral so as to not betray the sudden flash of fury tensing his muscles.

"Accepted?" She laughed, a joyless, brittle sound that bounced off the dining room's high ceiling. "No. 'Encouraged' is the word I'd use."

"Your mother? Another adult? No one stopped this?" Her story moved around the pieces he'd jammed together to solve the puzzle of Ruby Macintosh—spoiled mobster's daughter, jewel thief, and manipulative liar—leaving him with curved peg to fit into straight hole.

"Is that how it worked when you were growing up?" she asked, a knife-sharp edge to her question. "You had a mummy and dadums who loved you and looked out for you? Not all of us were so lucky."

An image of his mother with a belt tightened around her upper arm until her tired veins pressed against her pale skin flashed in his mind before he could drive it back into the darkest recesses of his subconscious where it belonged.

Focus, Bendtsen. Don't let her drag you down that path.

He folded his napkin in half and then half again before placing it over his empty plate. "You managed to get away from him. Why not make a clean break?"

"Do you really think I got away?" She rubbed her thumb over the initials etched into her palm as if it was still healing. "That would be a good trick."

"You're saying you didn't?"

"No, he simply indulged my wish to leave until he decides that he won't anymore."

Now *that* fit in with the information in her file. Rolf Macintosh was like a spider with a very large web. He'd let the little flies roam out to the edges, but he'd never let them go.

"What does he hold over your head?"

"The only two people I love." She let out a long, shaky breath, her chin trembling and her shoulders slumping forward for a fraction of a second before she snapped back up and replaced the moment of vulnerability with a blasé expression so bland it bordered on hostile. "My brother, well, you know all about Jasper and his determination to work his way up to become my father's right hand man. As for my mother, she's…not herself. She's totally dependent on him for everything, so when he asks for information, an introduction, a favor, I have no choice but to say yes, or they will pay the consequences."

If he didn't have a long list of people who'd been robbed or died under mysterious circumstances after meeting with her, he'd be sympathetic—or as close as someone like him could get to that. "And murder, is that something you're forced to do?"

"Oh yes, that's right." She toyed with the mix of long silver and gold chains that lay draped across her cleavage, her gray eyes mocking him when his gaze made it back up to her face. "I'm a bejeweled black widow."

"Did you kill them?" It was a stupid question to ask, never let a target know even the slightest bit of doubt existed, but the words were out before his brain had a chance to filter them.

She shrugged her shoulders and then took a drink of wine, watching him over the edge of her glass as if she couldn't believe he'd asked the question so many simply wondered about silently or whispered about behind her back. Whether that was a good or bad thing—and why he even cared enough to wonder—he couldn't pin down.

"In a way, I'm as responsible as whichever of my stepfather's lackeys actually did the deed," she said as she sat her glass down. "I know the rules. I have my freedom, but it's limited. You'll have to watch yourself if you're going to make it off Fare Island. Rolf picked out my future husband years ago, and it's not…" Reaching over to the folder, she flipped it open and ran one pink-tipped fingernail across the name written there. "Luc Svendsen."

"The others, the ones who died or were robbed, were your lovers?" The idea bothered him more than he wanted to admit, even to himself.

"Some of them. Then I realized what my father was doing, and…dating lost its appeal." Ruby closed the folder and pivoted in her seat so she faced him and tilted her head to one side before raising an eyebrow in question. "What makes you think the same fate won't befall you once you step foot on my Fare Island?"

He could tell her, explain about Luc, the man he used to be—the one he brought out when the need arose, the one who'd turned into exactly the kind of man all the social workers in the juvenile system had predicted he'd become if he didn't straighten his life out. Instead, he pushed his chair back and stood up. The less she knew about how much truth was in that folder, the better—for the operation's chance of success and his own sanity.

"Read the file, and you'll find out exactly why Rolf Macintosh will welcome me with open arms." Without waiting for her inevitable questions, he turned and strode to the door. However, he couldn't shake the one question that had been gnawing at him as he tried to piece together the new puzzle of Ruby Macintosh, so he turned back toward the table where she sat, her hand resting on the unopened folder. "Your brother is an adult, he's made his choice about participating in your father's business. Presumably your mother has made her choice to stay with him as well. If you want to go, why not just disappear and leave them all behind?"

She started in her chair and blinked in surprise. For a second, he didn't think she was going to answer him, but then she shook her head slowly and something that looked a lot like pity crossed her face.

"I take it back," she said, her voice soft and a little sad. "I don't think mommy or daddy did love you. If they had, you wouldn't have had to ask that question."

Venom. Frustration. Snark. All of that he expected and could take. The brutally honest mirror she held up instead threw him off stride. A flash of defensive anger sizzled up his spine, and in a split second, he was once again the scrawny kid in worn hand-me-downs who hated the world. The rush of fury felt good, like the best kind of powerful high that was *almost* worth the nasty, bone-snapping hangover when he came down. But he wasn't that kid anymore—he never would be again—so he squeezed the emotion into submission.

"We leave first thing in the morning, you have until then to memorize everything in the folder," he said, the words clipped and precise. "And remember what I said in my study. You try to sabotage this operation, and I'll make any threat your father has made to you look like a love letter."

Elskov had saved him from becoming Luc Svendsen. Now, Lucas Bendtsen would save it right back.

Chapter Four

Ruby didn't realize her stomach could fit inside her throat, but there it was gagging her as the small four-passenger plane hit yet another air pocket, jiggling her in her seat as Lucas piloted them closer to her own personal hell.

Fare Island sat in the middle of the North Sea, a green and gray oval of lush grasses and stony fjords that jutted out into the deep blue, daring the water to try to break it. Her stepfather couldn't have chosen a better headquarters for his operation. Out in the middle of miles of water, dotted with unexploded ordnance from World War II and the occasional shark, it wasn't a place the uninvited would stumble upon. Its isolation made government surveillance difficult, always a bonus when negotiating the sale of kilos of cocaine, arranging transport for human smuggling, or selling caches of arms to the world's despots and thugs hell-bent on doing serious damage. As the island grew bigger in the jet's front window, all she could think about was that here she was, right back where she'd started. No matter what, she never could shake the place for long. Even with all of the shit that came along with it, Fare Island was home—a criminally dysfunctional home populated by the twisted and the deranged, sure, but home nonetheless.

The slash of white cutting through an otherwise green scene came into view. The landing strip was well monitored and only a few miles from the main house.

"We're cleared for landing." Lucas's voice came in through her earphones. "We have to operate under the assumption that someone is watching and listening at all times. Our objective is to uncover the time and location of the arms exchange, which is expected to go down soon, so the Silver Knights can be in position and stop it. If you have questions about the plan contained in the folder, about how we'll do that, or our cover story, now is the time to get them out."

The Luc Svendsen she'd read about in the file last night wasn't her father's equal, but he was a right bastard of a powerful villain who dealt in secrets and blackmail. The treasure trove of scandalous information he supposedly had access to would be unbearably appealing to Rolf—and he'd be willing to kill to gain access to it. The idea of Lucas ending up on the wrong end of her stepfather's 9mm shouldn't bother her. Hell, it would be karmic justice. Still, she couldn't squash the bitter unease building inside her.

Confusion about his cover or the plan wasn't the problem. She was certain that it was all going to go horribly wrong. "What about concerns?"

"Keep those to yourself."

She bristled, her uneasiness gone in a flash of annoyance. "You know, you really are an asshole."

His eyes were hidden by the reflective aviator sunglasses, and a day's worth of dark scruff roughed up his jawline. Still, he didn't have any problem letting her know exactly what he thought of her statement when he turned his head and grinned at her. "Abso-fucking-lutely."

If her stomach had been in its rightful spot, it would have done a loop-de-loop at the cocky badassery of the smirk. As it was, her pulse started dancing the conga and a flush warmed her cheeks. Dammit, he shouldn't be able to unsettle her like this.

Unsettled? Is that what we're calling it?

Ignoring the question that could only lead to total idiocy, Ruby turned her gaze back to the island runway. As the plane's tires touched down on the tarmac, she let out a deep breath and focused on what really mattered. Not the asinine attraction toward the man in the pilot's seat, but on her commitment to surviving the next few days so she and Jasper could finally be free of her stepfather's poisonous talons and the Elskovian Silver Knights' schemes because neither of them would let her or Jasper go after this operation.

If everything went wrong, her father would kill them without a second thought. If everything went right and the Silver Knights were able to stop the arms deal, they wouldn't want to let her go. Her stepfather had his hands in enough other criminal enterprises that that she and Jasper would make valuable secret operatives. She'd be a double agent for the rest of her days with Jasper's life hanging in the balance.

There had to be a way out. She just had to find it.

• • •

Standing inside the jet's open doorway, Lucas glared at the brick wall of a man standing at the bottom of the plane's steps blocking their path. Dressed in head-to-toe black like a comic book villain, he didn't have a neck, an ounce of body fat, or a visible weapon. Taking the goon down wouldn't come without a lot of pain, but it could be done. Lucas had done it before, but he wasn't going to this time. In addition to the probable snipers with their guns trained on him at that moment, he needed to let this play out. The plan wasn't about force. It was all stealth.

"Claude, how nice to see you again," Ruby said from a few steps behind him, her voice polite but cool.

The 'roided-up goth kept his focus zeroed in on Lucas. "You know Mr. Macintosh doesn't like surprise visits."

Using the cover of his aviators, Lucas scanned the area, searching for the telltale glint of the sun hitting a rifle scope. He clocked two on the roof of the hanger. In addition, a man almost as large as Claude stood next to a Jeep parked at an angle on the tarmac.

"Don't worry," Ruby said, coming to stand next to him on the narrow step. "He'll enjoy this bombshell."

Claude didn't move.

Alarm bells clanged out a Hosanna in Lucas's head and he tensed.

Ruby just did that hair toss thing women did that could either be a come-on or a challenge and stared down Claude. "Let me introduce you to Luc Svendsen."

The giant raised a bushy, brown eyebrow in recognition.

"My fiancé."

The other eyebrow shot up.

She slipped her arm through the crook in Lucas's elbow. "I'm hoping you won't spoil the surprise for us. I'd like to tell my father the good news myself."

Claude's eyebrows went back to their starting position, and he pivoted so they could pass. He pressed a finger to the nearly invisible comm unit in his ear. "All clear. Stand down."

Ruby slid her arm down his and intertwined their fingers. As soon as they passed Claude, she let out a shaky breath and followed Lucas's lead toward the black hardtop Jeep waiting a few feet away. Attraction sizzled its way up his arm, the slow burn wasn't something he could chalk up to being on operation-ready alert. He'd gone undercover as Luc too many times to count over the years and women had always been present to solidify his cover as a player, but the extra sensory *awareness* of another human being hadn't happened before. The fact that it had now, with her, pissed him off.

He opened the passenger door and pushed the seat forward before helping her into the backseat. The Claude clone had moved from standing beside the Jeep to sitting in the driver's seat. Ruby slid across the backseat, the move raising the hem of her flowy, white skirt to mid-thigh. The flash of creamy flesh had his dick arguing with his head.

Lucas had two choices: in the back next to her, or shotgun where he'd have access to the door. The argument against the door being that on this island there was nowhere to run if things went ass up. The argument for the backseat being that he'd be next to Ruby and her distractingly delectable legs. He let the passenger seat slide back into place and got in the front row. It wasn't a chicken move. It was about situational awareness and control.

Whatever you have to tell yourself, Bendtsen.

Without a word to either of them, the driver took off down the single-lane road toward the main house. Lucas didn't bother to try and hide his curiosity as they sped down the road. Noting the details of the gently sloping terrain and the guards posted along the dirt road fit in with his cover. Luc was many things; a trusting idiot wasn't one of them.

Neither, it seemed, was Rolf Macintosh. They'd no sooner stepped out of the Jeep in the gravel, circular driveway in front of the stone house ten minutes later, than guards were patting them down. He expected this treatment for himself but cut a sharp look toward the guard sliding his palms down Ruby's side.

"I told you, Luc, there's no place like home." An old bitterness clung to her words, but she didn't resist the search.

After a few minutes, the guards stepped back empty-handed. No doubt there were others searching his plane top to bottom, looking for weapons or anything else of interest. They wouldn't find anything. Not that there wasn't a small armory on board, but he'd designed the secret compartments himself, and there was no way any of the thick-necked goons would find them.

"Mr. Macintosh is waiting in the house," their driver said.

"Thank you." Ruby raised her chin and took Lucas's hand.

The sizzle was back, zipping up his arm and giving him thoughts that had more to do with finding her naked and spread out on his bed, than with discovering the coordinates of the illegal gun exchange that would give Gregers Henriksen all the firepower he needed to launch a guerrilla assault on Elskov.

His first instinct was to pull away, but that couldn't happen, not when the front door opened, revealing Rolf Macintosh standing in the foyer looking every bit like a blond, buff, aging action-movie hero. Next to him stood a man as dark as Rolf was light. Joey Brotzka glowered at Lucas. As good with his left hand as his right when it came to guns or knives, he'd started out as muscle and worked his way up the food chain to become Rolf's number two.

Ruby tensed beside him. Glancing from the woman at his side to the man looming behind Rolf, Lucas realized his fiancée hadn't told him everything. Something was definitely off here.

"I understand congratulations are in order," Rolf said as he led them through the foyer and into the living room, not looking back, simply expecting them to follow.

Two armed guards stood inside the doorway. A flash of silver underneath Joey's black blazer when he crossed to the fireplace meant at least three shooters in the room. Taking a casual look around, he noted the solid red light above the video cameras mounted to the ceiling and the Glock lying in the center of the large wooden desk. After that, the less important details came into focus. The room was a jarring contrast to the man standing in the middle of it. Dressed in all black just like his lackeys, Rolf was the biggest dark spot in the sunny room filled with muted yellows and pinks dotted with an explosion of the soft, feminine touches of ruffles and flowers.

Ruby slipped from his grasp as soon as they'd walked through the double doors, her white skirt swirling around her long legs. Now she stood a few feet away with her hands planted firmly on her hips as she glared up at her stepfather. "Claude never could keep his mouth shut."

"You know how I am about surprises," Rolf said with a noncommittal shrug of his shoulders. "So does Claude, and *he'd* rather not get on my bad side."

A charged silence filled the room—and not an unusual one judging by the bored expression on the guards' faces. Still, he couldn't miss the dark-red flush blooming at the base of Rolf's throat or the way Joey gave him a hard look before adjusting his blazer so the butt of his holstered handgun could be seen clearly.

Dickwad.

Knowing he had to play this with just the right amount of attitude and acquiescence, Lucas gave Joey a taunting wink before turning to his pretend future father-in-law and holding out his hand. "Mr. Macintosh, it's good to finally meet the man behind the legend."

The older man took his hand in a grip that crushed Lucas's knuckles together and cut off circulation to his fingers. Lucas didn't blink. Apparently satisfied that he'd delivered his message, Rolf ended the pulverizing handshake.

"A flatterer, Ruby?" he asked, playing up the disappointed

stepfather role, even though he had to know exactly who and what Luc Svendsen was. "I never would have expected."

"Maybe you make him nervous," she said.

"As I should." Rolf paused and looked Lucas over as if he were a used car he was considering buying. "Then again, Luc has quite the reputation himself, especially for someone so rarely seen in person or photographed. Is it true you got ten million euro out of the Luxembourg royal family?"

And just like that the pieces clicked into place. No doubt the old man was already seeing the possibilities for his outfit if Luc came on board. Rolf had all the muscle he needed, but in today's world, information was often more powerful than a punch to the gut, and the old man knew it.

"I can neither confirm nor deny that," he said, letting his smirk do all the talking.

Rolf clapped a hand on his shoulder. "A man who deals in stolen secrets has to have discretion."

"It is our stock in trade," Lucas agreed.

"I admire a man who knows when to hold his tongue." He narrowed his eyes at Joey, seemingly sending a specific message to his second-in-command, then turned his attention back to Lucas and gave him another friendly pat on the back. "So you fell for my little girl, eh?"

Lucas glanced at Ruby, the sunlight playing across her pink, purple, and blond hair, and softened his expression. "Yes, sir."

"You didn't think to ask my permission before you proposed?"

The trap wouldn't have been any more obvious if it had been in neon. "Would your daughter have said yes afterward if I had?"

Rolf laughed, the sound booming in the room, as he walked with Lucas to Ruby's side. "You do know my little spitfire well." He took his daughter's left hand and held it up.

"Where's the ring?"

Lips compressed into a line, Ruby tugged her hand free. "I'm designing it now. You know how picky I can be, *Daddy*."

The vein in Rolf's temple pulsed, and he flexed his jaw. Ruby tensed at his side. Warning sirens blaring in his head, Lucas laid his palm against the small of Ruby's back, pressing gently against her and rubbing the pad of this thumb in slow, small circles as time stood still. Finally, millimeter by millimeter, she relaxed into his touch.

"I guess that's the trouble with marrying a jewelry designer," he said, keeping his tone as light as the mood was heavy.

Rolf slid his flinty gaze over to Lucas. There was more than just annoyance there. He couldn't pin it down, but whatever it was, it made Lucas's fingers itch for the cold comfort of his 9mm. Then it was gone and the proud papa was back.

"Well then," Rolf said, strolling over to the nearby liquor cabinet. "The only thing left for me to do is to pour some drinks so we can toast the newest member of our family."

He poured a clear liquid into three small glasses and handed one to Ruby and then to him. The sweet and spicy, slightly peppery scent of caraway wafted up from the glass. Akvavit. The Macintoshes may not be Elskovian by birth or geography, but had clearly adopted some of his country's customs if they toasted with the national drink that would put even the best vodka to shame.

"To the happy couple." Rolf lifted his glass in toast.

Lucas and Ruby did the same before downing the akvavit in one swallow. It burned its way down his throat, bringing back memories of other toasts with criminals just as depraved—if not as successful—as the man he faced. None of them had ever known that the man with whom they toasted would destroy their organizations from the inside out.

"Have you two set a date?" Rolf poured another shot of

akvavit into each of their glasses. "Your mother will want to know."

"Not yet." Ruby's fingers tightened on the tiny glass until her knuckles paled. "How is she?"

"Much the same, but this news will cheer her up." He lifted the glass to his mouth but stopped before it reached its intended target. His jaw went slack, and he let out a throaty laugh as he shook his head with wide-eyed wonder. "You know what? You should get married here at Fare Island this weekend. There's nothing like a wedding to cheer up your mother."

Lucas choked on the akvavit, searing his esophagus in both directions.

Ruby spoke up. "I don't think that's—"

"If you're going to get married anyway," her father interrupted, steel threading through his words. "Why not do it here and make your poor mother happy?"

The words hung in the air as Lucas ran through the scenarios in his head. Say no and the jig could be up. The old man was suspicious. He'd have to be an idiot not to be. They didn't need him to be a true believer; they just needed him to believe enough to let down his guard the slightest fraction.

"It's Monday. We haven't done any planning." The words tumbled out of Ruby's mouth in a rush. "I don't even have a dress yet."

His brain continued to spin as he watched the tension grow between stepfather and stepdaughter. Say yes and he'd find himself married, under his legal name, Luc Svendsen, to a woman known—rightly or wrongly—as a black widow and expected to become part of the family business in some shape or form. Divorce was a given, but that came with complications of its own for his cover.

"Mere details that shouldn't matter if you are *really* in love and *truly* ready to make this kind of commitment," Rolf countered with a wave of his hand. "I can fly in Antoine Alstar to design a one-of-a-kind wedding dress, and Father Simon is always happy to come visit. It's the perfect plan, unless you aren't ready to make an honest man out of Luc here."

On the surface, it was typical banter, but there was no mistaking the pressure building in the room. Even the guards had lost their bored expressions watching one of the most feared men in Europe being openly defied. The angry red splotch was back at the base of the old man's throat. There wasn't any more time to consider his options.

"Let's do it," Lucas said before he had time to second-guess himself.

Ruby whipped her head around to face him. "Are you serious?"

Time to sell it. Taking her chin between his thumb and finger, he tilted her head upward. Anticipation snapped between them like a live current. "Without a doubt."

He dipped his head. Her gaze softened, and her lips parted. Later he could justify it to himself as necessary for the farce they were playing out in the middle of a dangerous den of thieves, but at that moment, he couldn't lie to himself. He had to taste her. Before he could close the distance between his lips and hers, she spoke.

"As long as we can find Jasper so he can be here for the ceremony. It wouldn't be the same without him." Triumph flashed in her eyes for a moment and then was replaced with the besotted look of a woman in love. "Could you use your connections to find him on such short notice and get him to Fare Island for the wedding?"

Bloody hell. She had him by the balls, and she knew it. Unlike him, she hadn't given in, even momentarily, to the tug of attraction between them. That fact should have frozen the hungry heat spiraling through him. But nothing about him seemed to work right when it came to Ruby Macintosh.

"For you?" He dropped his focus to her very kissable mouth. "Of course."

Her eyes widened in belated realization of his plans, and she let out a soft gasp, but it was too late.

Taking advantage of the moment, he brought his lips down on hers in a swift kiss. He swept his tongue inside her sweet mouth, teasing her while tormenting himself with a taste of something deliciously forbidden and undeniably needed. He ended the contact, pulling away before he got lost in her.

"That settles it, then," Rolf said, the slightest trace of doubt woven into his tone despite his beaming expression. "We have a wedding to plan."

Chapter Five

Lips still tingling, Ruby clicked the sturdy door to her old bedroom shut behind her and leaned against it. She'd been gone a year and yet nothing had changed in her room—except for the addition of the man who'd turned her world upside down. All brooding bulk and testosterone, Lucas looked out of place in such a frilly room with its soft pastel colors, ruffled pillows, and yellow beechwood furniture. However, here he was with her father's approval since they were, as he put it, getting married in a few days.

Before he'd gone all caveman on her downstairs with that showy kiss that had delivered more punch than expected, she was confident she had the upper hand. Now, with him prowling around her room, she wasn't so sure—and they weren't even through the worst of it yet. Dinner would bring its own complications. She needed to keep her head clear and forget about that kiss if they were going to make it out of what was sure to be a clusterfuck without blowing their cover story.

"We'll have to change for dinner." She strode to the large

armoire and opened the doors. As expected, someone had brought their suitcases from the plane and unpacked them. No doubt they'd done a thorough search before hanging a single item.

"You look fine to me," Lucas said, but he wasn't even looking at her.

His attention was focused on a cell phone with one of those thick battery cases as he circled the room. She'd never had trouble getting a cell signal in the room before and was about to offer him her phone when the truth hit her. He was sweeping the room for listening devices. She wasn't sure if she was more pissed at her father for possibly bugging the room or at herself for not thinking of it first.

He circled the king-size bed with its sky-blue duvet and the two cream chairs set in front of the fireplace, then moved on to the oversize armoire and uncluttered vanity table while the device let out a series of quiet beeps. Finally, he slid the phone into his inside jacket pocket and turned to glower at her.

"Are you completely fucking insane?" he asked in a harsh whisper.

The answer to that depended on who was answering, but she didn't think he really wanted a response to his question. "I guess that means the room is clean of bugs."

He wasn't going to be put off though, judging by the way he stalked over to her, predatory intention clear in every step that brought him closer. Her pulse shot up, and every instinct warned her to run, but she stood her ground as he bore down on her. He stopped less than an arm's reach away, frustration dipped in desire pouring off him in waves that set off an answering, delicious shiver up her spine.

"Asking me to bring Jasper here." He shoved his long fingers through his dark hair, ruffling its perfect order. "You *know* that isn't possible."

"We both know it *is* possible—anyway, it's smart for you. It lets you flash a little of that Luc Svendsen magic that has Rolf all hot and bothered." She snorted at his surprised look. Men always were ready to believe anything about her, except that she could add two plus two and get four. "Oh yes, I know that despite what your written plan stated, I was just your invitation to Fare Island. The really big bait you're dangling so he'll let you in close, is the possibility of learning all the secrets you have about the influential people he wants to control."

"I don't need Jasper here to prove that I'm valuable."

"No, you need him here to prove that you're willing to make sacrifices for the organization. He knows it will cost you valuable favors to get Jasper here. If you don't think he has some inkling that my brother is in custody, then you vastly underestimate him." Too many people had tried to influence her father by currying favor with his family. However, neither her mother, brother, nor she had a direct line to her father's heart. "That's what he really cares about. Until you can prove your value to the organization, you're an interesting distraction."

She was right. He'd have to be an imbecile not to realize it, and Lucas Bendtsen was no idiot. Like her, he stayed focused on obtaining the goal at all costs, no one who wasn't that way would have said yes to her stepfather's asinine idea to get married right away. They didn't have much in common, but they had that, even if their goals were at opposing ends.

"And the fact that having Jasper here will make it that much easier for you two to go AWOL didn't factor into your decision at all?"

Of course it did, but she didn't need to confirm it for him to know that. "What's wrong?" she asked, her sharp question softened by her teasing tone. "You think you can't beat me at the game you created and made all the rules for?"

His answering smirk made her pulse hop. "That's not

even up for debate."

Had they started flirting? Because it totally felt like they'd moved from fighting to flirting considering the way her lungs had shrunk and her nipples had peaked. Did Mr. By The Book even know how to flirt? His eyes darkened before he dropped his gaze to her parted mouth, then ever so slowly brought his attention back up. Breathing became difficult.

Yes. Yes, he definitely did know how to flirt.

"Good, then you'll get Jasper here and everyone wins," she said, unable to hide the slight, breathy tremble in her voice as she reached over and yanked the first dress she happened upon off the hanger sight unseen.

He glanced down at the dress in her hands and mumbled something that sounded a lot like bloody hell before looking back up at her. There was enough heat in his eyes to melt her on the spot. She held on to the silky material as if it were her last lifeline to sanity. "Now turn around. I have to change."

He didn't move. She *couldn't* move. The air sparked around them. Just when the scales started to lean along with her body toward him, he turned away. For a second all she could do was blink in shock as she stared at his ramrod-straight back and his hands clasped behind him.

Smooth move, Ruby. You're one tough chick all right.

She tossed the dress over the open armoire door and then unzipped the side closure of her skirt and let it fall down to the floor.

Let's try not to orgasm next time he makes eye contact, okay?

Her cashmere sweater went next. It wasn't until she was standing in her matching silver lace bra and panties that she realized which dress she'd grabbed. The Silver Knight agent who'd packed her clothes while she'd been locked up at Moad Manor obviously didn't realize the amount of under rigging the silver dress required. With the deep V back, a bra was out of the question since she didn't have the backless bustier she normally wore with it.

She grabbed the front clasp of her bra, but hesitated. She could swap out dresses. There were other options in the armoire. Switching was tempting, but she couldn't do it. Maybe it was immature, but he'd seen her take this one, and she wasn't about to change because the thought of being without a bra around him sent a wave of warm desire flooding her core. She wouldn't give him the satisfaction.

Her gaze flicked over to Lucas who stood with his back to her, his broad shoulders so tense it looked like they were about to snap. He was probably pissy because she'd gotten the drop on him with Jasper.

Taking comfort in that, she unsnapped her bra's front clasp. Lucas's shoulders went impossibly taut. That's when she noticed him watching her in the small vanity mirror's reflection. The one-foot-high oval looking glass wasn't enough to let him see all of her, but obviously it was enough. Averting her gaze as if she didn't know he was watching, she slipped off the bra, slower than necessary, and took her time getting the dress down from where it hung and sliding it on.

Temporary insanity? Most definitely. Amazingly hot? Without a fucking doubt. If he was any other man, she'd have him naked and between her legs by now—as it was, she'd be fantasizing about Lucas with his face pressed to her slick folds for years to come.

Knowing there was nothing she could do about her pebbled nipples pushing against the silver material, she smoothed her hands over her hips to stop from reaching out for him. "You can turn around now."

He did, moving his hands as he rotated so they were clasped in front of his upper thighs and groin. If there was a reason for that, it didn't show on his face. His expression was as hard as the stiff cock he couldn't quite hide.

The vein in his temple throbbed. "I need to make a call."

"It's okay, I still need to do my hair." Not trusting herself not to reach out to him, she gave him a wide berth as she crossed to the vanity.

"I need to make this call in private."

"I see." Trying her best to keep her hands steady, she opened the vanity's top drawer, pulled out a hair clip, twisted her hair into a quick chignon, and fastened it. "Well then, I'll see you in the dining room."

Without waiting for his answer, she hustled out of the room before she gave in to the arousal making it hard to remember exactly who Lucas was and exactly what they were doing on Fare Island.

• • •

Lucas unfurled his fists and let out a deep breath that did nothing to alleviate the stiffness in his cock. He didn't mean to look at Ruby while she changed. He *shouldn't* have looked, but he couldn't have stopped if there'd been a gun to his head. Ruby Macintosh screwed with his head—both of them. And worst of all, she was right.

Bringing in Jasper would be a show of might and ease whatever doubts lingering in the old man's mind. Of course it also came with a huge downside. What would Jasper say when he got to Fare Island? For the past forty-eight hours he'd been holed up in a safe house with a team of agents. Jasper was a shit human being—except for his devotion to his sister. Just as they'd dangled his incarceration in front of Ruby, they'd done the same to Jasper. Now he had to weigh the benefits of increasing his value to his target against the total crapshoot of having Ruby and Jasper in the same airspace while forcing them both to keep their mouths shut about what was going on.

It was a brilliantly insane move, and it *would* work.

He punched in his clean contact number, one that was routed through several call stations and wouldn't link him back to the Silver Knights, and slipped his Bluetooth into his ear so he could talk while changing into one of his suits already hanging in the closet.

"Hello." Sgt. Talia Clausen answered on the first ring.

His shoulders relaxed an inch or two at the absence of the word "sir" from her greeting. To anyone listening in, either to him in the room or via devices that picked up both sides of the transmission on his cell phone, it was just a greeting, but it meant that there hadn't been any trouble at the safe house.

"You wouldn't believe how much turbulence there was on the flight over. It reminded me of that time going over the Alps. Also, I need you to look into something for me on the quiet. I'm doing a favor for Rolf Macintosh and need you to put the word out that I'd like the location of his son, Jasper. Seems the boy hasn't made an appearance in a while."

He paused in the act of buttoning his shirt hoping the sergeant would be able to quickly translate the code for her to accompany Jasper to Fare Island right away. She'd have to make clear to him the consequences of letting out any information about his recent circumstances.

"Consider it done. Does the jet need to be checked out before you go up again?"

Relieved at her quick understanding, he resumed buttoning and considered her suggestion to bring in backup. They had a team an hour away by jet. It could be done—but not yet.

"It's probably not a big deal. I hope the next time I take my bride up in it she'll have a better experience."

"Are congratulations in order already?"

"Yes, Ruby's father had the great idea for us to have the ceremony here." And with that, he delivered the update that the sergeant would translate and report to the queen.

"Will you be needing anything for the ceremony that I can send along?"

He knotted his dark blue tie. "No, I have it covered."

There was already a small armory hidden in the smuggler cargo bays on the plane he'd flown to Fare Island.

"Of course." She paused and the sound of shuffling papers came in clear over the line. "Before you go there was a message for you from Ms. Olsen."

The queen had spent ten years in New York City hiding in plain sight as a stylist named Elle Olsen, a common enough surname in Elskov. He'd argued she needed a different code name, but the queen was a stubborn woman. "What does it say?"

"That Mr. Colt has an appointment with another firm and can't commit."

Shocked, he pushed the Windsor knot up too tight on his neck and had to take a second to loosen it. Mr. Colt was Rolf Macintosh. And if he couldn't commit, that meant that someone from up high had declared him untouchable. The Americans? The British? Both were likely candidates to look the other way on some of Rolf's deadly deals in exchange for information that lead to juicier targets and headed off terrorist attacks. He couldn't blame them, but still the new information tied a double knot around his balls.

"That's too bad." Yeah, that was one way to put it.

"Indeed," Clausen said, only the barest hint of annoyance creeping into her tone. "Is there anything else you need?"

Something to go right before Gregers Henriksen got his hands on enough weapons to launch a guerrilla attack on Elskov.

Instead of voicing that thought, he said, "Just be sure to put the word out to my contacts about Jasper. We're working on a tight deadline with the wedding this weekend."

"Consider it done."

He pocketed his cell phone and strode out of the bedroom, noting the discreet security cameras perched high along the hallway and the obvious guards posted at frequent intervals as he made his way down the stairs to the family dining room.

Three courses later, Lucas sat at the formal dining room table trying to pinpoint any weaknesses in the Macintosh family dynamics that he could exploit in his search for the date and location of the arms deal. Rolf sat at one end with Joey on his right. The two had spent the entire dinner in silence. Lucas sat at the old man's left with Ruby next to him. At the other end of the table sat Ingrid Macintosh, who looked enough like her daughter to make the differences stand out. The nervous laugh. The flinches at unexpected noises. The fine lines around her tired gray eyes. The forced cheerfulness in her tone.

"So tell me, Luc," Ingrid said in her soft voice. "How did you two meet?"

The question yanked him out of his thoughts, and it took a second to realize what she was asking. It was just long enough to make the quiet of the dining room scream.

"At the corner coffee shop." Ruby took his hand in hers and brushed a kiss across his knuckles. "You know the one, Mom, right up the street from my apartment? I've texted you pictures of the funny signs they always put out front."

Ingrid blinked a few times, her eyes vacant, before something in her daughter's words seemed to catch hold and she smiled. "Yes. They had the sign about no wifi and having to talk to each other."

"That's the one," Ruby said. "Well, I went in one day and ordered a huge mocha not realizing that my wallet wasn't in my purse."

"So I picked up her tab." He finished her sentence as he draped an arm around the back of her chair, giving her shoulder a squeeze in thanks for how she'd covered for him.

She may not want to be here with him, and she was still trying to figure out how to hightail it off Fare Island with Jasper, but—for the moment—they were on the same team. The pinch in his lungs lessened, and for the first time since they arrived, he let himself relax.

"And how did you propose?" Ingrid asked.

"Nervously." He chuckled, playing up the part of the charming Luc Svendsen who never met a woman he couldn't put at ease.

"I can't believe you thought I'd ever say no." Ruby rested the back of her head into the pocket of his shoulder, looking every bit like a lovesick fiancée.

He shouldn't be surprised, considering that she'd grown up literally in a den of manipulative thieves, but she took to the subterfuge like a gold digger to a four-carat diamond. If only she'd been someone different, Ruby would be the perfect ally.

Ingrid dabbed at her eyes, a soft smile turning up the end of her mouth. At the other end of the table, though, Rolf and Joey didn't react at all. The two men were too engrossed in the smartphone lying on the table between them.

"That is just the most romantic thing." Ingrid's smile wavered, and she wiped at the wet spot under her eye. "I know that you two are a modern couple, but I do hope you're willing to adhere to a few old traditions."

He fidgeted in his seat. "What did you have in mind?"

She withdrew a long, thin gift-wrapped box from next to her plate and handed it to Ruby, who opened it. Inside was a long silver chain, a heart-shaped lock, and a key.

"What is it?" he asked, already knowing by the ashen tint to Ruby's face that he wasn't about to like the answer.

Instead of answering right away, Ingrid stood and walked over to them, a pair of scissors in her hand.

"First, you'll need to remove your suit jacket and shirt,"

she said as if it was a totally normal request. "Don't worry, that's the extent of how much you'll need to disrobe now."

He looked around the table. Someone had to object to this bizarre request. Rolf and Joey barely glanced up from the phone between them. Ruby had suddenly become entranced by her wineglass. Ingrid gave him an encouraging smile. Not liking it one bit, he stood up and stripped off his jacket and shirt.

Oh yeah, this doesn't make you look like a jackass at all.

"Sorry about this, darling," Ingrid said as she used the scissors to snip the left shoulder strap of Ruby's dress, which miraculously stayed in place. "But trust me, it will make getting ready to go to sleep tonight so much easier."

Ruby gulped audibly but didn't make a noise of complaint.

Ingrid lifted the filigreed chain out of the box. "This is a hand-binding chain," she said as she encircled first Ruby's left wrist and then his right wrist so the chain formed a figure eight around their wrists. Then she clipped the lock closed and added a layer of warm wax around it that cooled almost instantly. "It's an old but honored tradition on the island to test a young couple's devotion to each other. If you can't spend twenty-four hours together before the wedding, then you may want to rethink your commitment. One of the servants will deliver special binding clothing in the morning so you'll be able to get dressed even when you're bound to each other. I'll remove the wax and unlock you after dinner tomorrow night. If you feel the need to have the binding undone before then, or if you break it yourself, then that will be a very bad omen for the marriage."

Lucas stared down at the deceptively sturdy chain tying him to Ruby as both of his heads fought about whether it was the best or worst thing to have happened today.

Chapter Six

Ruby had thought going to the bathroom while Lucas had faced away from her and stood as far away as the chain wrapped around their wrists allowed was as bad as it was going to get that night. She was wrong. Lying under the duvet in the darkened room pretending to be asleep next to him was worse.

Hours after they'd turned in, there was no relief from the persistent vibrating hum of her body reacting to Lucas's nearness. The accidental brush of his muscular calf against the side of her foot. The constant tingle dancing up her arm from the brush of the back of his chained hand against her knuckles. The low rumble of his breath that made her own lungs tight as his deep inhales dragged the thin sheet across her pebbled nipples. She'd never been more aware of every single part of her body than she was at that moment, and there wasn't a damn thing she could do about it.

"Please stop making that noise," Lucas said, his voice as smooth as warm honey.

Everything but her heart froze. That particular organ

went into overdrive as if someone had just jabbed her with a needle full of adrenaline. "What noise?"

Lucas rolled so he faced her, their chained wrists lying on the bed between them. The full moon sent just enough light through the bedroom window to highlight every one of the things about him she should be ignoring. The sheet had slipped down to his waist, giving her a clear view of the dusting of hair over his hard pecs and the happy trail that narrowed before disappearing under the covers. Her mouth went dry, and she jerked her gaze back up to his face. For once, not every dark hair on his head fell into perfect alignment. Instead, it was tousled and a shadow of scruff covered his normally clean-shaven jaw. His eyes glittered like aquamarine gemstones as he watched her with enough intensity to make her bite down hard on her bottom lip.

His body tensed. "That one, the one that sounds halfway between a sigh and a moan."

"You're hearing things." She hadn't made a noise. She would have realized. Okay, maybe she made a little huff sound, but only that last time. And it had been quiet, barely a whisper really. "I didn't make any noises."

He raised an inky eyebrow and smirked before propping his head up in his hand. The new position let him stare down on her and the look he gave her set a warm wave of desire rushing across her already primed body.

"Liar."

He delivered the single-word challenge with enough seduction in his tone that it took a second to register.

"What did you call me?" she asked, slowly enunciating each word fully and grabbing hold of the much more acceptable emotion of annoyance to stop her from giving in to the half-dressed temptation that she was chained to.

"I could have just told you your pants were on fire." He smirked. "However, you're not wearing any."

What a pompous, double-standard holding, blackmailing asshole. "I didn't see you keeping yours on."

No, he'd stripped off his pants without even giving her a warning to look away. It had taken an embarrassingly long moment for her to slap her free hand over her eyes to block out the sight of his thick, muscular thighs and high, round ass. Getting out of her silver dress had taken a bit more cooperation from him. After she'd struggled to get the zipper down, he pushed her hand away and lowered it for her. All of her attention focused on the bare brush of his fingers along her spine, the dress had slipped off, thanks to the snipped strap, before she could catch it. Putting on a nightgown or T-shirt was impossible while they were chained together unless she wanted half of it slung up on her shoulder. They hadn't spoken a word to each other as they got into the bed, which had seemed so much bigger the last time she'd slept in it alone.

He shrugged one of his broad shoulders. "I get hot at night."

"At least that makes up for how chilly you are during the day."

Now that was a direct hit.

"You think I'm cold?" he asked, the heat in his eyes at the moment anything but.

Keeping a grip on the sheet so it wouldn't inch downward, she rolled onto her side so she could deliver her next words face-to-face. "You're an ice floe on the winter solstice."

"Really?" The air sizzled between them as his gaze dipped down to her mouth and then traveled down her curves, burning a trail of fire across her skin as if the thin sheet wasn't even there.

Ignoring the warning bells going off in her head, she brazened on. "As if you're really shocked by that assessment."

"That's not how I'd describe what I'm feeling." He shifted

until he was close enough that the intoxicating heat coming off him washed over every inch of her. "Not even close."

Her breath caught. She should roll over, turn away, stop wanting—despite her every instinct screaming at her to get away—for him to eliminate the small distance between them. But like a lust-drugged idiot, she tilted her chin upward so only millimeters separated their lips. The moan escaped before she realized she was making it.

Desire darkened his eyes to the deepest shade of ocean blue. "There's that little sound of yours again."

Denying his statement wasn't an option. In the next heartbeat, his lips were on hers in an icy-hot kiss that didn't just silence her instinct to run, but turned it to ash. He deepened the kiss, his tongue plunging inside to tease and torment in the best possible way. The same rush of desperate wanting that had burned her from the inside out when he'd watched her reflection as she'd changed into her dress before dinner, returned with a vengeance. All of the pent-up frustration of lying next to him while she was wearing only her panties stole away her common sense. Every frisson of attraction since she'd walked up the steps of Moad Manor pushed its way to the surface.

Without ever breaking the kiss, she pushed him onto his back and rolled along with him so she sat astride him. The sheet tangled around their legs, locking them together just as the silver chain around their wrists did. She rocked against his hard cock, the lace of her panties and the cotton of his boxer briefs blocking direct skin-to-skin contact was as frustrating as it was tantalizing.

She planted her palms on his pecs and straightened up, breaking the mind-melting kiss while still undulating against him. Closing her eyes and losing herself in the passion and the electric sensations rocketing through her was the smart move, the trick she usually played with the men she dated. But this time, for whatever reason, she couldn't. She kept her eyes open and watched him. She drank in the sight of his muscles flexing and the way his jaw tightened in a pleasure and pain mix whenever she rotated her hips. It wasn't just that, though; it was the war of control playing across his face that fascinated her as much as the pleasure touching him gave her. Like her, he didn't give in. Ever. He would always find a way to get exactly what he wanted.

An unexpected bolt of emotional want slammed into her. Just the idea of what it would be like to be at the center of all that determined focus hit hard enough that she had to drop her gaze. But that wasn't her. She would never be that woman. Growing up like she had, she knew better than others the danger of that kind of obsessive devotion.

"We shouldn't be doing this." He ground out the words while letting his unchained hand glide up her side and then cup her breast before expertly rolling her hard nipple between his fingers.

"I know." But that didn't stop her from moving against his hardness, each forward and back stroke sending jolts of pleasure ricocheting through her core.

"It's just the situation." He curled upward and lifted her breast to his mouth. "The nearness." He grazed his teeth across her nipple. "It's you." He sucked it into his hot mouth while doing some magical circling thing with his tongue around it that had her clenching her legs tight against his hips. He released her nipple with one last flick of his pointed tongue. "I'd have to be dead not to want you."

If he'd meant his words to put her off, to add distance between them, it wasn't going to work. Not now. The draw was too strong, too undeniable.

"Rationalize however you can, but you want this. So do I." And she did—more than anything else at the moment. The rest of the world, the chaos of the next few days, the danger that surrounded them like a high-voltage spider's web as long as they were on Fare Island, none of it mattered.

The air around them changed the moment he'd made his decision, almost as if there was more energy in the room than it could contain. With a muttered curse, he sank the fingers of his unchained hand into the flesh of her hips and pulled her tight against his girth so she couldn't help but feel every inch of him against her heated flesh. When she began to move against him again, it was amazing their underwear didn't spontaneously combust.

"You like this, do you? You like rubbing that sweetness of yours against me. You're so wet for me, so hot." He sucked in a quick breath. "Do that again."

She shouldn't play with him, not when they were both on the edge, but she couldn't help it. She wanted to see him go over that line he was always so sure never to cross.

"This?" She twisted her hips, the move dragging the damp center of her panties over and exposing her slick folds.

"God yes." He tightened his one-handed grip on her hip and arched, grinding against her.

It was good, it was so fucking good, but it wasn't enough. Before she could even take the time for a plan to form, she shot up and stood on the bed over him. Their chained-together hands hung in midair between them.

"I want you inside me." Fast as she could, she shimmied out of her panties and kicked the tiny swatch of material off the bed.

The vein in his temple pulsed. "Not yet."

Planting her hands on her hips, she glared down at him. "Why not?"

"I want to hear you make that noise again." He curled his hands around her calves and urged her up toward the headboard. "I want to hear it while my face is buried between those long legs of yours. I want to hear it while you come all over my tongue."

His fingers tugged her down—not that she was fighting—until she straddled his face. The moment he lapped at her wet center with his tongue, she stopped breathing. It was a soft tease of a touch that had her white knuckling the beechwood headboard with her free hand. The other hand swung loose until he pulled it around her back as he reached behind her, grasped her ass and pulled her core closer to his demanding mouth.

With each lick and twist of his tongue, with ever-deepening suction on her clit, she lost a little bit more of herself to the moment. She'd closed her eyes as the sensations bombarded her, but she still saw him. There was no distancing herself from him like she always had with her other lovers. There was something about Lucas that wouldn't accept that, and it had pierced her defenses. That made him more dangerous. It also made the vibrations building in her core stronger with his every caress. She couldn't stop the desperate moan that escaped as she gave in and let her head drop back.

"That's it," he said against her soaked, sensitive flesh, his fingers biting into her ass and holding her tight against his mouth. "That's the sound I want to hear."

The brush of his words against her folds followed by the rhythmic press of his tongue against her clit sent her spiraling over the edge. Her climax hit like a lightning bolt, sending waves of white-hot pleasure slamming through her and whipping her body taut. If it hadn't been for Lucas's hands holding her up, she would have collapsed on top of him.

Breathing hard, she sank down, twisting as she did so she ended up on the bed beside him. There were limp noodles with more bones than she had right now. Lucas didn't have that problem. Cracking open her eyes, her gaze immediately went to the outline of his hard cock pressing against his boxer briefs. Suddenly, she wasn't so tired anymore.

"Please tell me you have a cond—"

Thump!

Thump!

Thump!

"Open this door right now, Ruby," Jasper yelled through the door sounding as pissed off as she'd ever heard him. "You can't marry that asshole." He slammed his fist against the door again. "Open. Up."

Jasper? Here? It didn't make sense. Her brain was still floating somewhere outside her body, tossed out by the climax that had so thoroughly rocked her world. Then reality crashed through with the force of her brother's pounding fists. Jasper was here. Lucas had gotten her brother here.

"You were the one who wanted him on Fare Island, so you better find a way to control him before he fucks up this entire mission," Lucas said, his voice a harsh whisper. "I won't let that happen. Do you understand?"

All of the post-orgasmic haze evaporated in an instant as the reality of where she was and exactly whom she was with blasted through her. What had she been thinking?

Her brother pounded on the door again. "I will break this damn thing down, Ruby."

"Shut up, Jasper!" she hollered. "I'm coming."

"We're coming." Lucas held up his arm, dragging hers up with it thanks to the chain connecting them.

She glared at him and scooted out of the bed, leaving behind twisted sheets that smelled of sex, but not the man who'd helped her make them that way. The sooner she figured out how to do that, the better, because an attraction like the one between them was nothing but trouble.

Chapter Seven

Answering the door with a barely covered hard-on while chained to the woman whose taste lingered on his lips wasn't exactly the way Lucas had imagined this part of the mission going down. Then again, nothing had gone according to plan since he'd set eyes on Ruby Macintosh. He should be used to it by now, but it still made him twitch. A man had to stick to the plan, otherwise everything turned to shit.

Ruby grabbed her robe from the armoire, shoved her free arm through the sleeve and then tied it closed toga style so her chained arm remained outside of it. Then, she gave him an appraising look. As soon as her gaze dropped below his waistband, her cheeks went pink and her attention jumped back to his face. "Do you have anything you can put on?"

"I'm not a silk robe kinda guy."

Her lips twitched, but instead of the smile he expected, she let out a huff of frustration. "You have to put something on."

Considering the fact that her brother was already in mid-meltdown, it was solid advice. He scooped up his suit pants from where they hung over the armoire's open door and awkwardly tugged them on with his free hand. Tucking his protesting cock down one pant leg and zipping them shut took a bit of work, but he managed. Confident he looked completely ridiculous in slacks and a bare chest, even if slightly more appropriate, he opened the door.

Ruby's brother stormed through the opening, followed by Sgt. Talia Clausen, who looked as pissed as Jasper had sounded when he'd bellowed through the door. He was a big guy and had that whole crazed, mad-dog-ferociousness vibe going on. Lucas stepped in front of Ruby before Jasper could get within arm's reach, blocking her from a possible — if improbable, going on the siblings' history — attack. The move put his chained arm behind his back, but he wouldn't need both arms to kick Jasper's ass if it came to that. The guy was as tall and bulky as his sister was petite, but it would take someone a helluva lot bigger to get through Lucas to hurt Ruby.

The woman in question, however, had other plans. With a swift shove from behind, she moved in alongside of him. Jasper glanced down at the thin silver chain connecting Lucas's and Ruby's wrists and muttered a few choice curses before letting out with something much, much louder. "What in the hell are you thinking, Ruby?"

"That my *baby* brother needs to remember how to use his inside voice."

"Really?" he asked, his voice dropping a few decibels. "We're ten months apart, so you can stop the baby brother shit, especially when you're the one acting like an idiot. Do you even know who he is? He's with the — "

Lucas moved to smack the words right out of the other man's big mouth, but before he was even halfway to the target, Jasper grimaced and his whole body jolted straight for a second before slouching back to normal.

Jasper slapped his hand over the brand-new, small red welt on the side of his neck and glared at Clausen. "You have *got* to stop doing that."

Clausen, who stood only a few inches shy of Jasper's six-foot, two-inch frame, didn't back down. "It's set to the lowest voltage rating, and it was only for a second." She pocketed the Silver Knight's prototype stun gun, disguised as a flashlight, that she'd just used to shock him. "Anyway, I warned you what would happen when you wouldn't stop ranting on the jet."

"And I told you what would happen if you zapped me again."

"She's done this before?" Ruby took a threatening step toward Clausen, had more than half a foot of height on her, not to mention some of the best fighting skills of the Silver Knights.

Lucas raised an arm to put a roadblock in Ruby's path at the same time Jasper sidestepped in front of the tall, redheaded Silver Knight. It was probably to protect Ruby, but Lucas's sixth sense said otherwise. Yet another thing he'd have to have a word about with one of his best agents.

"Who are you?" Ruby asked while pushing against the barrier of his forearm.

Like a good agent, the other woman remained cool. "Clausen. I'm with him." She nodded toward Lucas.

Before Ruby could ask any of the 482 questions he could practically see rolling through her head, Lucas held a finger to his lips. He'd swept the room for listening devices before dinner, but hadn't since they'd returned. Clausen closed her mouth immediately. Jasper and Ruby wore matching outraged expressions but didn't utter a word.

He crossed the room with Ruby in tow, the silver chain taut between them, stopping at the armoire and taking out his shave kit from the shelf above the hanging rod. "Look, Jasper, I know I'm not the guy you expected your sister to fall for. I'm sure that like your dad, you'd hoped she'd pick Joey."

He took out what looked like a smartphone, but was actually an RF signal detector that could detect any listening devices and most wireless cameras. He continued to ramble on about how he and Ruby were perfect for each other as he and his intended circled the room checking for bugs. Finally, when no alerts popped up on the screen, he laid the device down on the vanity table. Now they could get down to it.

"Bring me up to speed, Clausen."

"Do you want to go somewhere more secure?" She looked pointedly at Ruby.

"Well, since we're currently chained to each other." He lifted their connected wrists while Ruby shot an annoyed look at him that did nothing but make him want to kiss her until she again made that little moan she made only a few minutes ago. "I don't think that's possible."

Jasper grumbled under his breath and glared at Lucas.

He did not have time for this. "However, *little brother* needs to wait in the hall. Quietly."

"That's not gonna happen." Jasper took a step forward, the look in his eyes just daring Lucas to try and move him.

The ego on this one was unbelievable. Lucas stuffed down his natural, inborn instinct to beat some respect into the drug-dealing asshole. "You're our prisoner, or did you forget the two kilos of cocaine we found on you?"

Clausen cleared her throat. "There's been a development, sir."

His stomach twisted. God, he hated developments.

"I stay," Jasper said, cocky satisfaction written all over his smug face. "Ruby gets off this island as soon as we can get that chain off her wrist."

Lucas's blood pressure skyrocketed. "You're not in the position to be calling the shots."

"Actually, the United States government says that I am."

"Bullshit."

"It checks out, sir," Clausen said.

Lucas whipped his attention over to the Silver Knight agent. She had the tense, pinched look on her face of a woman about to go before a firing squad.

"I got back channel confirmation on the flight over here," she said. "He's with the agency."

Of all the explanations she could have given him, that was the least expected. He mentally scanned over the brother's and sister's files until he hit on the one factoid that made it all make sense. Rolf Macintosh wasn't their biological father. That honor went to a low-level gangster in New York. They'd been born in the United States and therefore had dual citizenship. Add to the mix the fact that every governmental spy agency from the Kremlin to Washington and everywhere in between wanted to keep tabs on Rolf Macintosh's criminal empire, and the CIA turning Jasper into a protected asset made perfect sense.

"You're sure." He already knew the answer, but had to ask.

Clausen nodded.

"Are you fucking kidding me?" Ruby said, her words so soft they barely registered, even if the amount of fury pouring off her could be measured onto the Richter scale. "I agreed to this whole farce to protect *you*."

The smart-ass slid off Jasper's face, replaced by a softer, more concerned look. "Rubes, how many times have I told you that I don't need your protection anymore? You, however, are in way over your head. You can't be here for what's about to go down."

She crossed her arms, yanking his connected wrist over so it lay against the knot of her robe. "What exactly is that?"

"The less you know the better," Jasper said.

Her brother may have known Ruby for his entire life, but

even after only a few days, Lucas knew she wasn't going to let go that easily.

She jerked her chin up. "I already know about the gun sale."

"Jesus. Are you trying to get her killed?" Jasper glared at Lucas, his gaze dropping to Lucas's arm held out at an awkward angle. "Or just get some entertainment while you search for the date and location of the exchange? She's not one of us. She doesn't know the rules. She could get hurt—or worse."

It took everything Lucas had not to look over at the twisted sheets on the bed. What happened to Ruby after the operation was finished wasn't his concern. He had to focus on keeping Elskov safe. The mission didn't have room for anything else. Still, he moved over so not even a fraction of light could get between them.

"That's not going to happen." He wasn't fooled by the bored look on Jasper's face as he looked between them and then the rumpled bed.

"Oh really?" Jasper asked when his attention landed square on Lucas.

"Dammit, Jasper," Ruby hissed. "I'm not an idiot."

"No," Jasper said, his voice low and tight. "You're just a cover."

Ruby stiffened. "Something I agreed to so I could clean up after one of your messes again."

"Me getting caught wasn't an accident." Jasper shoved his fingers through his hair. "I needed to make contact with the Silver Knights, and I figured with the arms exchange coming up, they'd fall for the cocaine in the trunk hook, line, and sinker. Which they did."

The only thing in life Lucas hated more than being taken for a fool was the watery split-pea soup he'd survived on when his mother was still alive. A setup. He'd built his entire carefully considered plan based on a setup.

"He kept his mouth shut about all of this until we left for Fare Island. At that point, I couldn't get him to shut up," Clausen said from her spot by the door, her hands clasped behind her back, and her back straight in the Silver Knights version of at ease.

Brain spinning, he ran through the possibilities. They were still there. He'd have to figure out how to mix the interfering Americans in on this operation, but he'd find a way to keep it minimal.

"What's the CIA's interest in this?" he asked.

"Same as yours," Jasper responded. "We have to stop the exchange."

"There is no 'we.'" No. There was Elskov and then there was everyone else.

Jasper shrugged. "You'll have to take that up with the U.S. government because that's who I take my orders from."

Since killing him and dumping the body out the window wasn't an option, Lucas ground his teeth together as he enjoyed the mental picture of Jasper sailing through the midnight sky without a parachute.

"How long?" Ruby asked, her voice shaking just enough to yank Lucas back to the here and now.

Jasper's mouth formed a tight line, and for a second it didn't seem like he would answer, but he did. "They recruited me when I was on my post-university trip to New York."

"That was *years* ago." Ruby's gray eyes widened with shock. "You never told me."

"I couldn't. Anyway, if you'd known what I'd been doing for the past five years, you would have worried more. I know you."

"At least one of us can say that," she snapped.

"Rubes." He reached out for his sister, but she rebuffed the attempt. "Don't be that way. I didn't have a choice about telling you."

The benefit of growing up as a foster kid meant his family drama was of a different shade than what he was seeing between sister and brother. For him, hate was just hate and neglect only neglect. But the animosity and hurt building between Ruby and Jasper had a different feel to it, the kind that would sink this operation if he didn't get them to stop now.

Lucas spoke up. "We only have a few days to find the location of the exchange. Do you have leads?"

"Nothing beyond that it's supposed to happen this weekend. The betting money is on Sunday. Rolf doesn't trust me enough to give me details, so it's a good thing I'm such an amazing snoop." Jasper said. "As much as I hate this marriage ruse, at least it got me back on the island so I could track that information down—even if I had to bring along my latest flavor of the week."

"Just what I always dreamed about being called." Clausen rolled her eyes in disgust. "Finally, after working my ass off in the academy and then Silver Knights training, my dream has come true."

"Then we start tomorrow," Lucas said, already sorting out a plan that took the new factors of Jasper and Clausen being on Fare Island into account. "We have to get the location of the exchange."

"It's gotta be on his phone," Jasper muttered.

Rolf had the phone fisted in his tight grip when he'd greeted Ruby and Lucas after they'd arrived on the island. At the dinner table, the crime boss had only briefly looked up from the glowing screen during the meal as the phone lay between him and his right-hand man. Even the recon photos of Rolf the Silver Knights had on file showed the phone.

"He does seem attached to it," Lucas said. Too bad the simplicity of the answer didn't make the solution any less complex.

"His life's on that fucking thing," Jasper said, rubbing the spot on his neck where Clausen had zapped him. "It's encrypted, secured six ways to Sunday, and you'd need your own personal army to peel it out of his grasp."

Lucas shrugged. "Sounds simple enough."

Jasper looked at him as if he were delusional. He wasn't. He was just determined not to let anything stand in his way. This arms deal could not happen. He had to figure out how to do that without outing Jasper, blowing his cover, endangering Ruby, or violating the queen's edict not to harm Rolf Macintosh. A child's game for a guy who'd figured out how to navigate the foster system by the time he was seven, survive on the street by the time he was thirteen, and play for the good guys when he joined the Elskovian army at eighteen.

"Just remember that—" Jasper pointed at the chain at connecting Lucas's and Ruby's wrists. "is just pretend. Don't fuck with her because you think you can. I know the truth about you."

"No one is fucking with me," Ruby said, getting right in Jasper's face. "But you sure are pissing me off."

"Rubes, you don't know him. He's not who you think he is."

Lucas couldn't argue with that. It was, after all, exactly how he liked it.

"Oh, stuff it." Ruby jammed a finger into her brother's chest. "I'm a big girl and can take care of myself."

She whirled on the ball of her foot and turned to face Lucas. The glint in her eye screamed out trouble, but before he could do anything, she'd raised herself up on her tiptoes, cupped his face in her hands, and planted her lips on his. The kiss was like a triple shot of akvavit on the first day of winter. It burned in the best way and blasted the rest of the world to smithereens. It was total madness—the kind he'd always sworn off—but ignoring her sweet tongue as it begged for entrance into his hungry mouth wasn't an option. The moment he opened his mouth and invited her in, the tone of the kiss changed. Shock and awe melted away in the face of such heated need on both their parts. Then, as fast as it began, it ended with her hand moving down to his chest and pushing him away and turning back toward her brother.

"Now get out of here before the Sparrow realizes you're wandering around after-hours," she said, her chin high and gray eyes gleaming.

"Too late," her brother snipped. "I already told him I was giving Talia the grand tour."

"At three in the morning?" Lucas asked, still trying to get his bearings back.

Jasper shrugged. "I sold it."

"He pretended to be drunk," Clausen said, her hand on the bedroom doorknob.

"Then be sure to sell it on the way back to your wing," Ruby said.

Jasper stalked over to the door, stopping right as Clausen opened it. He turned back to stare down Lucas. "Remember what I said."

Hating that her brother was right to warn Ruby off him, Lucas fell back on the best defense mechanism any kid from a fucked-up background had: exaggerated sarcasm. "Don't worry, if I was wearing shoes right now I'd be shaking in them."

Taking the initiative, Clausen stepped outside the door and let out a simpering, tipsy giggle. "Nighty night then, lovebirds," she said in a singsong voice and then tugged Jasper out into the hall with her before closing the door behind them.

The silence after all of the noise of the last twenty minutes bore down on him. Ruby's shoulders slumped, and she lifted a palm to the back of her neck and rubbed. The urge to replace her touch with his own and comfort her was as overwhelming as it was misplaced. He couldn't give in, but he wasn't a total monster. What had happened between them before her brother barged in hadn't been just for their cover, but it couldn't happen again.

"Ruby—"

She held up a hand and shook her head. "Just don't, okay? Let's chalk it up to strange circumstances and forget about it so we can concentrate on getting the information you need, so I can get the hell off this island and away from every lying, manipulating one of you."

That should be all he wanted. It *was* all he wanted. So why did her dismissal sting so much? After doing an awkward shuffle scoot to get back onto the bed and under the covers, he laid his head down on the pillow that still smelled of her lust, knowing that would be the one question he really didn't trust himself to find the answer to.

Chapter Eight

Ruby refused to open her eyes. The sunlight stabbed at her closed eyelids, making its presence known no matter how desperately she tried to cling to the last echo of her dream— one that involved Lucas and his big cock. There hadn't been even a hint of her brother going all battering ram on the door in the hazy non-reality of her subconscious. It had been a *very* good dream.

For at least a little bit longer she could deny the sun warming her cheeks, but there was no ignoring the sinewy arm curled around her waist or the hard, thick length of her dreams pressing against her ass. She was tucked firmly against Lucas, both of them on their sides. Judging by the cool morning air against her skin, the silk robe she'd tied toga style because of her chained arm had shifted up. The material had inched its way up to her hips, and the tie had loosened so the front hung open. Torn between adjusting the material and the lure of this peaceful moment, she inhaled a shallow breath to keep from waking up Lucas.

"I know you're awake," he said, his voice low and rough

with sleep.

Keeping her eyes closed, she snuggled down deeper into her pillow. "No, I'm not."

"Okay, then you go ahead and keep making that little moan sound you were doing a little while ago." He tightened his hold, pulling her more firmly against him. "Good dream?"

Her cheeks burned with a prickly heat. She didn't need a mirror to know how red she'd flushed. "Nightmare. All of the men in the world had teeny, tiny dicks."

He chuckled, blowing a few strands of her hair forward so they landed across her cheek. "That must have been horrible."

Blocking out the tickling of her hair, Ruby kept her eyes closed. Opening them would mean she'd have to acknowledge his closeness. She'd have to roll out from underneath his arm and relinquish that unnamable something keeping her warm that had nothing to do with the heat his strong body generated under the covers. Jasper was an ass, but he was right about Lucas. He wasn't the man for her, no matter how good he felt curled around her. She was the crime boss's daughter that he was blackmailing for access to Fare Island. He was the leader of the Silver Knights, devoted only to Elskov, who lied, cheated, manipulated, and killed to protect it. Growing up surrounded by thieves and murders, she'd had enough of that whatever-it-takes-to-win mindset to last a billion lifetimes. All she wanted was a little slice of truth, somewhere peaceful to lay her head, and the knowledge that the people she loved were safe from Rolf's vindictive reach.

Of course, knowing that didn't lessen her reluctance to crack open her lids and let reality come streaming through.

"Someone delivered the special hand-binding shirts half an hour ago," he said.

Her heartbeat picked up. "Who?"

"The Sparrow."

Of course. She should have known. "What did he say?"

"He didn't." Lucas drew the loose strands of her hair back and tucked them behind her ear, setting off an electric current of want that had her biting her bottom lip. "He just glared at me and dropped off the shirts."

She could picture that. The Sparrow was short, thin, and ever vigilant. The only things he seemed to hate more than strangers was a dull knife or an enemy who died too soon.

"Don't take it personally," she said, a smile tugging at her lips. "He looks at everyone that way."

"Except you."

True. She'd always been the exception that proved the rule. Well, her and her mother. Jasper had always been up to too much trouble, talked too much, and played too many tricks for a man like the Sparrow to put up with.

"He was practically my governess growing up."

"You had a governess?" Lucas asked, a teasing disbelief lingering in his words.

"I had something better. I had the Sparrow." She'd learned early on that there was more to her father's number one enforcer than appeared. He'd had a soft spot for kids, never met a stray animal he didn't want to adopt, and was a fabulous teacher, even if the skills he was imparting weren't exactly age appropriate. "I could pick a lock by four, hit a distance target with a throwing knife at eight, and by ten, I could get to every cave and hideout on the island undetected."

"And you decided to be a jewelry designer instead of a ninja warrior?"

"The Sparrow is the one who gave me my first sketchbook."

All those blank pages just waiting for her to make her mark. The memory of her first taste of creative freedom blocked her throat with a lump of bittersweet hope. Until then, she'd never imagined being able to make her own reality away from her stepfather's watch. It was the best gift she'd ever gotten.

"You sound like you care a lot about a man who would do this to you." He pulled down one of her hands tucked under her chin, turned it palm up, and traced his thumb over the raised scar of the *M* and *I* carved into it.

Glad again for the protection of her closed eyes, she clenched her jaw tight and willed back the tears so quick to come. The sharp, slashing pain in her hand had been nothing compared to the agony on the Sparrow's narrow face as he'd pulled out his favorite blade and drew first blood.

"My father wanted to do much worse. The Sparrow came to my defense. It was touch and go, but my father agreed. Forcing him to be the one to actually mete out the punishment served a dual-purpose. Rolf isn't a man who forgives opinions other than his own."

"Why did he defy your father?"

Were his questions a way to interrogate an asset? Probably. Still, the words came pouring out.

"The Sparrow has loved my mother for as long as I've known him. I think at least some of that transferred down to Jasper and me."

For a man like Lucas who only saw in black and white, the stream of grays that made up life growing up on Fare Island must be an anathema.

"Does Rolf know?"

She nodded. "He doesn't care. My mother isn't well. She's…" She paused, trying to think of a way to sum up her mother's fragility. The days she'd spend in bed. The constant dark circles. The listlessness. The air of hopelessness she'd always tried to cover with false cheer. "A little bit broken. Rolf considers her as his owned property. She'd never dare to cheat or leave him. Anyway, I think he enjoys watching the Sparrow's misery."

Her stepfather had found so many opportunities to throw the Sparrow and her mother together. Special guard duties on her shopping trips to Paris. Keeping her company on the days when she couldn't get out of bed. All of it with the unspoken threat hanging over both of their heads if they gave in to temptation. The man was a conniving tyrant, and he ruled Fare Island with an unbreakable fist. That was why she and Jasper had to break free for good. Her mother, she knew, would never go. Whatever bond held her tight to Rolf's side was beyond severing, but she and Jasper could do it. His connections in the U.S. could help them disappear. Even as pissed as she was at him for lying to her, she wouldn't walk away from her brother. Not now. Not ever.

For a while, she and Lucas lay quiet together. Maybe he was denying the reality outside this bed as much as she was. But, finally, he spoke.

"Why do you call him your father to his face if he's not? Jasper calls him Rolf."

Lucas's question yanked her out of their protective, pretend cocoon. She opened her eyes, the sun temporarily blinding her to her surroundings. Then, she blinked and the world fell into place around her. Fare Island. An arms deal. Blackmail. Her best chance at freedom.

"For the same reason he always finds a reason to keep the Sparrow near my mother," she said as she threw off Lucas's arm and sat up. "To remind him of what he does not, and never will, have."

• • •

Half an hour later, Lucas found himself struck dumb in the dining room.

Quick wits were his most prized skill. It was what had gotten him from being the neglected child of an addict to being at the point of the spear when it came to keeping Elskov safe. He'd always depended on them, used them, exploited them.

Looking at the twenty-five pictures of floral arrangements spread out before him, his wits fled him like a rat jumping off a sinking ship. Lives on the line? He could come up with a workable plan in heartbeats. But this? He had nothing.

"What do you think? Which one speaks to you?" Ingrid asked from her position behind his and Ruby's chairs at the dining room table.

Glancing back at her face, rapturous as she clapped her hands together and looked at him expectantly, his still half-empty stomach grumbled. He flashed her a quick smile that probably looked as fake as it felt before turning his attention back to the photos. The images lying above his plate of rye bread, cheese, and jam looked like those find-what's-different pictures where you had to find the sixteen differences between two almost-identical photos. "They all look nice."

Ingrid's mouth firmed into a line and she let out a quiet, if distinct, exasperated huff. In her defense, it was the twelfth time he'd uttered those words since he and Ruby had walked into the dining room expecting breakfast and finding Operation Wedding's HQ instead. Next to him, Ruby covered a quiet, better-you-than-me giggle with a bite of cheese.

Lucas struggled for something, anything, else to say about what looked like an explosion of feminine fluff around him. From the photos of the flowers to the different colored fabric samples to the fifteen options for wedding programs to the tasting slices of possible wedding cakes to the list of hairstylists, it was like Ruby's mother had whacked open a wedding piñata that had dumped out everything over the dining room table. How she'd managed to pull it all together in less than twelve hours escaped him, but it was a logistical and supply line miracle impressive enough to make him wish he could recruit her into the Silver Knights.

"Mom, give him a break," Ruby said, rescuing him once again from a total brain breakdown. "Number one, he doesn't know a marguerite daisy from a red clover. Number two, we just came down for breakfast twenty minutes ago, we're barely awake."

It was the most she'd spoken since they'd left the bed, tossed on their special hand-binding accessible shirts, and hurried downstairs, hoping for breakfast before everyone else in the house had woken up. They'd been greeted by a full buffet of breads, cheeses, jams, and coffee as well as Ingrid in her wedding-planning glory.

"I suppose I'll take that lack of sleep as good news." A faint blush turned Ingrid's cheeks pink, but she powered on. "But with only a few days until the wedding, we don't have time for you to be sleepy. Your father is insisting on only the best for your big day. He's already sent out the call for everyone to attend. I hate the lack of invitations, but there really just wasn't time. You know Rolf, lots of activities, trips, and plans had to be moved around so he could be here for the wedding. He can delay, but some things can't be postponed forever."

Lucas forced himself not to react to that bit of intel. Their information was that the exchange with Gregers Henriksen would happen soon, within the week. Instead of checking out flowers, he should be searching the grounds, breaking into Rolf's study, figuring out how to tap into the encrypted phone the crime boss never took a step without, but it looked like there was a possibility of gaining something out of breakfast after all. All he had to do was prod Ingrid a little.

"It can be crazy," Lucas said, keeping his voice light as he picked up one picture, pretending to examine it while he was really watching Ingrid. "Did he have a trip planned for this weekend? I hate that we made him rearrange his schedule."

"No, thank goodness," Ingrid said, anxiety pulling her features taut as she placed a shaky hand on Ruby's shoulder as if to steady herself. "He has a very important off-island meeting early next week, but Saturday's festivities will be over before he has to go."

Ruby's head snapped up. "Who with?"

"Some man named Gregars, I think. Or was it Gandry? You know me, always forgetting these things." She chuckled and shook her head. "This is why your father never tells me anything. I just forget."

The photo crinkled in his tight grip but he schooled his face not to betray the frustration bubbling to the surface.

Ingrid peeked over Lucas's shoulder at the picture he held. "Oh, I so agree. The rose and orchid bouquet is the perfect one." She squeezed her daughter's shoulder. "And you thought he wouldn't have an opinion."

"Where is Rolf?" he asked, being sure to keep his tone casual as he laid the photo on the table, smoothing its bent corner flat. "I should apologize for upsetting his schedule."

"Oh, don't you worry about that," Ingrid said, crossing to her chair and sitting down in front of her uneaten breakfast. "He loves the chance to throw around his weight a little and get people to jump to his command." Her tone was joking, but the teasing didn't reach her eyes which had lost a little of their spark. "Anyway, he's locked up in his study with Joey for the day. The good news is Antoine Alstar should be here in a few hours to start your dress."

"So soon?" Ruby asked, keeping her gaze locked on the bits of breakfast she'd pushed around her plate instead of eating.

"It's Tuesday," Ingrid said. "Saturday is only four days away."

The clock was ticking for Elskov. If the Americans were right, and he had no reason to doubt them since their information in the past had always been spot-on, the exchange was supposed to have happened this week. The question was, had the wedding moved the timeline up or pushed it back?

Either way, he didn't have time to waste on flowers and ribbons.

"Mom, you know you've always been so much better at all of this planning than I am," Ruby said. "I'd like to be able to show Luc a bit of the island, not to mention take a shower, before Antoine and everyone else shows up and things get crazy."

Disappointment and hurt flashed across Ingrid's face but disappeared almost so fast, he could convince himself he'd been mistaken if it hadn't been for the way Ruby flinched next to him. The door opened, and a painfully thin man with sharp, glaring eyes and a murderous expression walked in. The Sparrow was back and he was pissed.

. . .

Ruby should have expected it. The Sparrow wasn't one to pussyfoot around anyone, not even her father. That made him not only rare but a one-of-a-kind commodity on Fare Island. Add to that the fact that he was the closest thing she'd ever had to a protector, and she couldn't do anything but sit there with her mouth sealed shut as he stalked into the dining room.

The Sparrow took one look at all of the wedding paraphernalia and let out a snort of disgust. "I don't like it."

Her mother sighed. "Now, Hamish."

Hamish? She'd grown up with the man and had never known his first or last name. Everyone simply called him the Sparrow—except, it seemed, for her mother.

"I know it's not my place to say, but somebody has to." Like always, his gaze pinned her to her spot. "I thought you were getting out. Marrying this one just pulls you in even deeper."

Not telling him this *was* her escape from this life seemed like a betrayal, but she couldn't, not yet, maybe not ever. The guilt stole the words from her mouth.

"You say that as if you don't appreciate the kind of life we live," Lucas said as he toyed with one of the emerald fabric swatches with his unchained hand, letting the silky material slide through his large fingers.

Everything about him seemed calm, from the placid look on his face to the nonchalant slouch of his shoulders, but it was a lie, a con. The orgasm last night and all the talk of the wedding must have twisted together inside her because despite the visual proof to the contrary, she couldn't help but feel the conflict pulling at Lucas. He may not think he was a good man, but he was an honorable one, and the lies he had to tell were starting to take their toll. It must be difficult to only see in black and white in a gray word like theirs.

"It's good enough for me and you," The Sparrow snarled. "But not her."

"I know that," Lucas said.

The quiet, simple response made the Sparrow ratchet up his volume. "Do you? I know all about you and the things you've done to get where you are. You use people and leave them struggling to survive wherever they happen to land. You're a cold-blooded bastard without a heart."

The material Lucas had been toying with slipped from his hands, and he straightened in his chair, fury coiling his body tight. The Sparrow dropped a hand to the knife sheathed on his thigh.

It was as if the world stopped rotating. The only sound in the room was the blood rushing in her ears. "That's enough," she said, her voice a stone weight, slicing through the air in the tension-filled room. "You know his reputation, but you don't know him."

The Sparrow's tone softened. "And you do?"

Did she? Her brain said no, but some underlying, more primal instinct said she did, that they were more alike than either of them cared to admit. "I do."

The Sparrow opened his mouth to respond but the dining room door burst open before he could. Antoine, dressed in head-to-toe orange strolled in with a three-person entourage, oblivious to the tension sparking in the air.

"Madame and Mademoiselle Macintosh," he called out in his truly horrible fake French accent. "I cannot express how excited I was to receive the call. You know how I adore weddings, even the last minute kind."

"I'm so sorry about that." Ingrid quickly got out of her seat and hustled around the table to the designer. "But you know what a hurry young love is always in."

"That it is." Antoine delivered a pair of air kisses to Ingrid and then turned to face Ruby and Lucas. "Now stand up, my dear, and let me get a good look at what we have to work with."

Surrendering to the fact that her life was becoming one awkward moment after another, she sighed and stood up. Because of the hand-binding chain, Lucas stood up with her, taking her hand in his like a good fraudulent fiancé should. What wasn't fake was the sizzle of desire that rushed across her skin from even that simple act of intertwining her fingers with his.

Antoine's gaze dropped to their joined hands, and his face light up with joy and he clapped. "I *love* that you are following the old traditions. Oh the stories I've heard about what happens during the hand-binding."

"It was supposed to stay on until dinner, but obviously we'll cut that short so you can get what you need from Ruby for her dress," Ingrid said, her words spilling out in a rush as the two talked as if Ruby and Lucas weren't even in the room.

"We can't have that," Antoine exclaimed. "We will work around the hand-binding, and after I get the measurements, we can send the happy couple on their way to do whatever it is they want to do while I sketch a design."

Chapter Nine

An hour later, Lucas couldn't get the designer's words out of his head.

Whatever it is they want to do.

Lucas doubted the designer had meant suffering through tragic, brain-draining levels of sexual frustration staring at the thin silver chain curled around the partially-opaque, glass brick wall separating him from where Ruby stood naked under the shower spray.

What Lucas should be doing at that moment was banging his head against a wall until he figured out a way to separate Rolf Macintosh from his encrypted phone long enough to get the location of the arms deal. Short of getting the crime boss to let the meeting information slip, which he was too smart to do, Lucas was circling the drain on ways to get the date in time to stop the exchange. He'd pressed Ingrid as much as he could for information, but she hadn't added anything. He had to think of something before it was too late.

That's what he *should* be doing.

Instead, he stood in the bathroom, gripping what was

probably the shredded remains of his special hand-binding shirt in one fist and holding one arm aloft inside the shower—the one chained to Ruby—while fighting every urge he had to touch the woman who was wet, naked, and within reach. He clamped his jaw down hard and finished grinding down the top layer of his molars. He couldn't see her, well, not exactly. Any time he stupidly opened his eyes, his gaze was drawn to the vague outlines of her body as she moved under the spray. His memory of last night filled in the details. The peach color of her nipples. The full roundness of her tits. The flare of her hips. The rise of her ass. The curve of her thighs.

That was it. His jaw wasn't the only thing aching. Shifting his stance to accommodate the tightness of his pants, Lucas stifled a groan. At least he meant to. Of course the bathroom's acoustics exaggerated his quiet, unfulfilled misery.

His chained hand jerked upward as if Ruby had tugged her arm closer to her body to cover it from prying eyes, and she gasped, as if she'd forgotten he was waiting outside the shower.

"Now who's the one making noises," she teased, unable to cover a husky tremor to her question.

Remembering that sound she'd made as she came all over his tongue made his cock jerk against the confines of his pants. Fuck. He never should have tasted her last night. Now he couldn't forget her sweet taste. She'd brought color into his black-and-white world. That was dangerous to his mission and his very precise, self-prescribed life.

The mission.

His life was only about the mission.

This one.

The next.

It didn't matter.

He was his work.

Without Elskov, he was nothing, a fact that had never

made him flinch until now, until Ruby.

He fisted the shirt tighter in his hand and squeezed his eyes shut to keep himself from watching the frustratingly vague glimpses of her through the glass blocks. "Are you going to be much longer?"

"Why?" Her arm connected to his moved again, stopping at the height of her shoulders and then slowly in broad circles lower. "Do you need time to set yourself to rights?"

The image of her washing herself, the soap bubbles covering her tits, clinging to hard nipples, sluicing down her belly to the soft, pink cleft between her legs. Set himself to rights? His cock ached, the tip already wet for her, and it took every bit of self-control to stop himself from barging into the shower, pressing her wet, naked body against one wall, and giving them both exactly what they wanted.

Set himself to rights? She knew better.

"I'm not sure I can do that while you're this close to me." Or farther away. He'd wanted her since she'd strolled past him into Moad Manor smelling like sunshine and looking like sin.

She stilled her arm for a heartbeat before taking it lower. "Watch out, Lucas, that sounded an awful lot like the truth."

"It slips out every once in a while." What was the use in denying his hunger for her when she'd see the truth pressed against his pants as soon as she stepped out of the shower? For that matter, why was he denying it? He opened his eyes and turned to face the glass bricks separating them, giving in to the want making his body tight and his dick hard. He could watch without touching, without falling. The entire world shrank down to the flashes of her creamy flesh, distorted as they were, as she turned under the warm spray. It didn't matter that the view was partially obscured. His brain filled in what was missing and his desire added in the fantasy.

She tilted her head back, the long column of her hair became a partially obscured multi-colored rainbow down her back. "Do you ever get tired of it? The lies? The pretending?"

Deflection came naturally. "I could ask the same of you."

"If you did, I would tell you I am tired of it. I'm tired of it all—the manipulations, fake emotions, hidden resentments, secret agendas." Weariness crept into her words, marrow-deep exhaustion at the bullshit of it all. "At least you were up front, in your own weird way, when you blackmailed me into coming back here."

"That's…" He searched for a word, but everything he came up with sounded harsh about her family, her circumstances, her life, and he drifted off.

She let out a wry chuckle. "Pathetic, I know."

The shower turned off.

His breath caught as he watched her wipe a palm across the glass bricks, clearing away some of condensation fogging them up. It wasn't a clear view, but her faint outline became more prominent. Cursing the still indistinct view, he couldn't look away.

"Can we be honest with each other?" she asked as she reached up, curled her hands around the length of her hair and squeezed out the extra water.

The warning sirens went off in his head, but he ignored them. "To a point."

She grabbed the thick white towel draped over the wall and rubbed it across her wet skin. "I won't see you again after this is over."

"No." The single word jabbed into him like an ice pick to the kidneys, and he closed his eyes against it, a reflexive move to block it out.

"Then see me now."

The taut line of the chain binding them became loose. His eyes snapped open. Ruby stood in front of him, the towel at her feet. A few stray drops of water clung to her creamy skin, calling out for his tongue to lick them up. The damp tendrils of her hair hung down past her shoulders and curled around her impossibly hard nipples, begging to be rolled between his fingers. All of that was mind blowing enough, but then his gaze managed to climb upward, and he saw the challenge in her eyes and the daring smirk curling her lips upward. God she was astounding.

"I always see you."

"Good." Her gaze dipped down to the outline of his cock. "Is all that for me?"

Tossing aside any pretense that this wasn't going to happen, that he was going to fight the attraction holding them together more securely than the chain wound around their wrists, he let the shirt drop to the floor. He held her gaze as he flicked open the top button of his pants.

"I don't know if you can take it all." But he wanted to see her try, needed to see her lips wrapped around him as she sucked him in deep.

Something sparked in her eyes at his acceptance of her challenge, and she shook her head while whispering a quiet *tsk, tsk, tsk*. She closed the distance between them and trailed her fingertips across the bare skin above his waistband.

"Why don't you let me get a good look at what I'm working with." She sank to her knees, sliding one palm across his length, the barrier of his pants practically nonexistent at the heat of her touch. "Oh, I'm going to need to look at this up close."

He went for his zipper, but she slapped his hand away. The defiance made his balls tighten. "Careful there, I can only be pushed so far."

"Don't worry," she said, her voice breathy as she inched his zipper down. "I know how much you value control." She slipped her hand into the waistband of his boxer briefs, taking them down millimeter by achingly slow millimeter until his cock sprang free. "I'll only push you to your limit, and then I'll nudge you the rest of the way into blissful oblivion."

Of course she would. Ruby wouldn't ever be satisfied with some, she wanted it all, and he wanted to give it to her.

"You're trouble."

She winked up at him. "The absolute best kind."

He believed it already, but then she proved it.

She gripped his shaft with both hands, her fingers firm enough to let him imagine just how tight she'd be when he finally buried himself in her, and her pink tongue darted out and circled his head. Keeping her big gray eyes focused on him, she did it again, this time lapping up the salty pre-come waiting for her. Pleasure shivered up his spine, and the world stopped spinning. When her tongue retreated and the tiniest bit of blood circulated back to his brain, all he could do was stare down as she did it again.

This wasn't just a blow job, not for either of them. They might spend the rest of their lives pretending for the rest of the world, but right now, this moment? This was for them, it was their truth.

Unable to keep his hands to himself, he wound his fingers into her wet strands of hair, so cool to his overheated touch. He didn't tug her forward or surge into her sweet mouth. Not yet. This wasn't a meaningless hookup or an adrenaline-fueled release. He would take, *oh God would he*, but not until he was sure the woman naked and on her knees before him was ready. Then he was going to show her what happened when someone tried to nudge him into blissful oblivion.

"So beautiful."

She did an undulating move with her tongue and, unable to help it, he tightened his grip on her hair. The approving hum she made around his cock made his knees buckle. He did it again, so did she.

"You like that, do you?" He fisted her hair, pulling down so she was forced to look up at him.

She nodded as she moved her mouth up and down his hard length, the motion and her answer adding to the heady anticipation live in the air.

"What else do you like? This?" Taking his time, he slid his cock into her mouth before pulling back and then repeating the process going deeper and deeper until he bumped up against her throat.

Desire darkened her gray eyes.

"Yes, you do." He released her hair, moving his palm so it cupped the side of her head. "Maybe if you're good, you'll get some more later." He pulled out of her, defying the delicious suction that sent jolts of ecstasy through him. "Right now I have other plans for you."

• • •

Lust, hot and sure, slid through Ruby, melting away everything except for Lucas and the dangerous promise in his words. The taste of him still on her lips, she took one last long lap from the base to the head before rocking back onto her heels and staring up at him. She had a damn good idea about what he had in mind, but nothing took the place of hearing the dirty words from his talented lips.

"What plans are those?" It was supposed to come out teasing but ended up breathless and needy, just like her.

He dragged the callused pad of his thumb across her bottom lip. "Total honesty. You want it, you ask for it."

"And you'll give it to me?" Desire pooled in her stomach and spread outward with its molten fingers touching her everywhere at once. "Whatever I want tonight."

One side of his mouth curled up in a cocky grin. "Exactly."

It was too much to accept. That's not how things worked with her, definitely not on Fare Island where most people only wanted something *from* her, not *for* her.

"Does it work the other way, too?" She stood, taking her time and sliding her hands over his thick thighs, past the indent above his hips that she couldn't wait to lick and over to his hard pecs. "Are you going to ask for what you want?"

She'd never wanted to hear a yes so badly in her whole life. And like an ass, he didn't answer right away. Instead, his gaze dropped from her eyes to her mouth to all points south before taking the lazy route back up. Everything about it was deliberately, maddeningly, deliciously slow, and it made her core clench with denied want. Finally, he reached out and touched her, a light caress of his fingers across her hard nipple, just enough to draw out a tortured moan.

His responding grin was all sex appeal and naughty promise. "It wouldn't be any fun if we couldn't both be honest."

"So…" She let the word hang in the electrified air between them as she stalked around him, trailing her fingers over his broad shoulders until she stood behind him. His beautiful ass called out to her hands, but he'd be expecting that. She raised herself up onto her tiptoes and nipped at his earlobe. "What do you want?"

His muscles quivered under her touch, the first sign that his control was close to breaking. "Everything." He took his wallet out of his pants and removed a condom before dropping it on the counter. "But you can start with taking my pants the rest of the way off and then turning that shower back on."

The urge to whip his pants down and drag him into the shower nearly overwhelmed her, but she couldn't give in. If he wanted to torture her with a sensual tease, she was going to return the favor. She floated her hands down his sinewy back, enjoying the play of his muscles, tense with the effort of staying still under her touch. Her fingers slid along the taut lines of his lean hips, the sound of his muttered curses followed by a harsh groan sending a rush through her. Right on the edge of too soon and too late, she reaching his waistband. Keeping her greedy fingers away from his velvety, hard cock was hell, but she couldn't, not yet. She lowered herself along with his clothes as she tugged them down his strong legs, giving in and letting her tongue trace a line across his high, firm ass, before standing back up and sauntering into the large shower. The wrist linked to his held halfway out of the shower.

Warm water rained out of the nozzle, not that it mattered. The heat Lucas was giving off would have warmed an arctic shower. Holding her hand under the spray, she turned toward him. "Are you going to come in and get me all wet?"

"We both know you already are." He slipped on the condom and strode into the shower. He was hard and rigid, everywhere from the tightness in his jaw to the hard line of his shoulders to the thick length of him she couldn't wait to have inside her. "Soft, slick, and waiting for me."

She couldn't deny it. Didn't even want to.

Water clung to his skin as he stared down at her with an intensity that sent a hot wave of desire through her, obliterating the rest of the world outside the shower stall. Never looking away from her, he lifted a hand but instead of touching her, he reached past her to the bar of soap resting in a niche. Amusement glittering in his eyes, he dropped the bar into her hands.

Of all the things he could have done at this moment, passing the soap was the last one she'd expected. She stared at the pale-blue bar and then back up to his vivid aquamarine eyes, made even more so by how the water had turned his dark hair black. "What? You want me to wash your back?"

"And the rest of me, but not my cock." He grinned.

The smart-ass man actually grinned at her and the glimpse at the ornery side of him just made her nipples pucker to painful points. She didn't know how, but one way or another she was going to get him back for this, even if she couldn't keep the smile off her own face.

"So you have a clean kink?"

"No." The teasing look in his eyes disappeared, replaced by something hotter, hungrier, and more than a little dangerous. "I want to see how long I can draw this out before you're begging me to slide my fat length between your slick folds and fuck you until you come so hard you scream my name."

Playing it a helluva lot cooler than her overheated, desire-drenched body felt, she arched an eyebrow and rubbed the slippery bar between her hands. "The only question is which one of us will be begging for that first."

• • •

Right up until the moment when Ruby rubbed her soap-covered palms down his abs, Lucas knew the answer to that question. As soon as she made contact, though, he realized it was only a matter of time before he couldn't take anymore of her teasing touches and had her splayed open and pressed against the wet tile.

"What's this from?" She circled the round scar above his heart.

"Hazing." He could still smell the burning flesh and taste the blood from where he'd bit down hard on the inside of his cheek to keep from uttering even the slightest groan of pain.

Her eyes rounded. "The Silver Knights do that?"

"No, the gang I joined in secondary school did." In his neighborhood, it was the best route for survival, so he'd taken it. And if it hadn't been for a short stint in juvenile detention, he would have probably died in that gang.

"And this one?" Her thumb traced down the three-inch jagged scar along his rib cage before following it up with a trio of butterfly kisses.

"Not dodging in time." Good thing he'd learned fast or

that first mission with the Elskov special forces would have been his last.

Her hands wandered down to his hips where her fingertips came close enough to his straining cock to make it ache but not enough to do anything about it, because for once, she was following his orders. The irony wasn't lost on him even as he fisted his hands to keep from reaching out for her. If he could touch her without ending up on his knees begging, he would, but that wasn't going to happen.

So instead of being able to distract her with a caress, he let her turn him around so his back was to her. Might as well get it over so he wouldn't scare her later. He knew the moment she saw his last birthday present from his mother. She let out a soft gasp and sketched a finger over the belt-width scar tissue that crossed from one shoulder to his spine.

"And this?" Anger and sympathy mixed together so completely in two simple words, but no pity.

"Another time." He forced the dark memories back into the hole they'd crawled out of and focused on the woman in behind him. "Are you going to soap up your favorite parts of my body or will you get the rest of me too?"

Her hesitation hung in the air, and for a second he figured she'd ask for more. Instead, her hands sailed down to his ass and she cupped both cheeks in her firm grip, sending a shot of lust straight to his dick.

"I think they're *all* my favorite parts." She slid her hands around to his hips and closed the space between them so her full tits pressed against his back. Her light touch was an agonizing glory against his skin. "I love these V lines you have above your hips." She walked her fingers down his thighs, every nerve in his body reacting in sync to her touch. "And these, fuck, a girl could spend her day just admiring them." Back up went her clever fingers to his abs as she kissed her way up his spine. "You should consider hiring these out for people to do their laundry on. And this…" Fast as lightning she encircled him and gripped him tight and snug. "Might be my most favorite one of all."

The slow stroke she followed her words up with, going from the base to his swollen head and then swiping her slick thumb over the drop of pre-come on the slit, made him go momentarily blind. The woman was good, too good. Another few seconds and he'd be begging her. That wasn't how he'd planned to have this play out.

Ignoring his body's protests and the utter lunacy of the act, he unwrapped her fingers from around his shaft. "You're not playing by the rules."

She tugged her bottom lip between her teeth and looked up at him through her thick eyelashes. "I think you get off on teasing me."

God did he. Watching that heated flush crawl up her skin and the way her nipples pebbled did something to him. Seeing her pleasure was almost as big a turn on as watching her go down to her knees in front of him and lick her lips before taking him into her tempting mouth.

"There are benefits to drawing things out and slowing them down." And he was quickly forgetting each and every one of them.

"Like what?"

She ran her fingers down his chest and traced the outline of his abs and then followed the narrow trail of hair down to the base of his cock, the whole time giving him a flirty dare of a look challenging him to stop her. No doubt, she thought that was all she had to do to make him give in and beg. If only she knew how close she really was to making him do just that.

"The benefits? How about this." He grazed the back of a finger over her almost-hard nipple, circling the nub with a knuckle.

She gasped and bit down on her bottom lip. He wasn't the

only one teetering on the edge.

"Or this." He dipped his head down and licked a water droplet from the hollow at the base of her throat before following its wet trail up the side of her neck to the sensitive spot behind her earlobe. Earlier she'd nipped at him, returning the favor was only proper.

He'd barely razed the edge of his teeth across her skin when she moaned, and he sucked the tender spot again. His balls ached. His dick was screaming at him. The caveman determined to claim her howled for more. Still, he wanted to take her higher.

"Definitely this." His fingers glided down her spine, over the curve of her ass and down to the back of her thighs.

She trembled beneath his fingertips. "Lucas." She called out his name in a desperate whisper.

In response to her plea, he curled his hands around the back of her legs, lifted her up so his cock nestled in the heat of her soft, wet folds, and pressed her back against the shower wall. "Without a doubt this."

Sensation ripped up his body at the same time that all of his blood rushed south. Good didn't begin to explain the feeling making his balls tighten in anticipation.

Ruby let her head fall back against the tile wall and her mouth opened. She moaned, *her moan* — the one that said she was close just from the pressure of his dick sliding against her core and bumping against her clit.

"You're making that sound again, Ruby. Are you trying to make me go faster?"

She nodded and rocked her hips forward, hard against him. "Yes."

"There's only one way for that to happen." He clamped a hand down on her hip, forcing her to stop. Yes, he was being an asshole, but she had to say it. She had to want it and go after what she wanted. For once, she needed to take what she needed and to hell with what was in it for anyone else. "You have to tell me what you want."

She didn't hesitate. "Fuck me."

It wasn't begging, but he wasn't going to parse down to the nitty-gritty when he was this close to heaven. "How?"

Ruby cupped the back of his head and jerked his face close to hers. "So well that I'll never forget it."

Now that was a challenge he couldn't wait to accept.

• • •

Ruby couldn't take it anymore. It was all too much. "Please, Lucas. I need —"

The word was barely past her lips when he slid into her, filling her up in one long, slow thrust that nearly took her over the edge into the beautiful abyss. He was everywhere, surrounding her. His hands on her ass. His mouth on her neck. His chest pressed against the sensitive peaks of her nipples. He stretched her, making her beg for more even though she wasn't sure she could take it. Then he moved, withdrawing and thrusting with exquisite, maddening slowness that had her whimpering in his arms.

"Does that feel good, Ruby?" he asked, his words hot against her skin. "Is this what you want?"

Want? It was too tame of a word for this. It wasn't mindless fucking. It was more. "God yes."

They moved together, the water pouring over their bodies, as time lost its meaning. Each touch, each kiss, each caress took forever and a heartbeat at the same time.

"I could get lost in you," Lucas said as he surged inside her. "You feel so good."

She couldn't describe how it felt. It was too much coming at her at once, building up with each slide of him in and out. It was agony and ecstasy twisted into electric vibrations that took away her ability to do anything but rock against him as she clung to his wet shoulders and cried out her desperation in unintelligible moans. Her whole world tightened to the point where they were joined and his voice as he whispered in her ear, urging her on and telling her to take what she wanted, all of it.

"You're close, you're wrapped so unbelievably tight around me right now." His hand dipped down between them, the rough pad of his thumb finding her clit, circling it and taking her past the point of no return. "That's it, Ruby. Let it go. Come all over me."

As if she could stop herself. Release crashed into her, rippling outward in titanic waves that washed away everything but the man she clung to as if her life depended on it.

"So." He thrust into her as her core continued to clench around him. "Fucking." Another slide into her until he was buried so deep there was no him without her. "Hot." A third stroke, deep and hard, and he came with her name a rough groan torn from his lips.

The world came back into focus breath by breath, a little bit at a time. The white tile. The warm water splashing against them. The steam fogging up the glass bricks surrounding the shower. Beyond that was the rest of Fare Island, her family, and the covert operation that had brought them here in the first place. It was amazing how something so close could feel so far away when she was in Lucas's arms.

The unmistakable sound of a cell phone vibrating against a countertop snuck its way into their hidden spot. His body stiffened. She'd never hated anything as much as she hated that fucking phone right now.

"Duty calls," she said as she lowered her shaky legs to the shower floor.

"Always." He released her and slipped out of the shower to answer the call, drawing the thin silver chain connecting their wrists as tight as the vice around her heart.

Falling for a guy like Lucas shouldn't be easy, but it was and that was beyond dangerous. So she wrapped a thick towel around herself as he stood naked, water dripping off his body, and his glower became darker with every word coming from the person on the other end of the phone.

For all of its shitty timing, the call couldn't have happened at a better moment. Nothing like a clear reminder that this was a mission for both of them, definitely nothing more. The sooner they got the information Lucas was after, the sooner she could escape Fare Island and leave it all behind her for good.

Chapter Ten

An hour later, Lucas stopped outside the closed dining room door. The hand-binding shirt itched. The lack of a clear plan of action to gain access to Rolf's phone gnawed at the back of his brain like a piranha with an axe to grind. And the woman next to him stole his breath every time he got a glimpse of her out of his peripheral vision. Clearly, this mission was going pear-shaped, and the more time he spent on Fare Island the worse it was going to get.

Laugher filtered out from underneath the closed dining room door. Ruby tensed beside him.

The news this afternoon meant the time for fun and games was over. Gregers Henriksen had been spotted in Spain for half a second before disappearing again. Elskov couldn't wait patiently for him to appear again in hopes of trailing him to the exchange. The bastard was too clever for that. Getting the information from Rolf remained the best option, even as volatile as the situation may be. That meant pushing forward no matter how much he wanted to protect the woman beside him from the danger of being caught.

Duty to Elskov came first. Always. Still, he took her soft, small hand into his rough one. "Got your game face on?"

Tension pulled her pasted-on smile tight. "I always do."

"Not always." The image of her coming apart in his arms flashed in his mind. "You seem to let it slip off in the shower."

She froze for half a heartbeat before pivoting to face him and walking her hot-pink-tipped fingers up his chest, leaving a line of sizzling want in her wake. "Are you flirting with me so I'll relax?"

"Yes." Maybe then he would, too.

Stretching up on her tiptoes, she brought her lips close to his ear. "You should try it sometime just for the fun of it."

"I'll keep that in mind." Along with a thousand other things he wanted to try with her naked and spread out before him.

"Here." She brushed her lips across his jaw then reached up and ruffled his hair. "Now, it looks like you've been up to something besides brooding and pacing since you got that phone call."

Is that what he'd been doing? Probably. Everything after that phone call had yanked him away from her and the earth-shaking certainty that came with being sheathed inside her warmth. The Silver Knights had confirmed Jasper's claims of being a double agent working for the United States government. An agent working as a liaison with the Spanish government had delivered the news about Gregers. So close. They'd been so damn close to getting the bastard, but, once again, he'd slipped right through their grasp. That couldn't happen again. They had to stop the arms exchange. God knew how many innocent people Gregers would mow down in his quixotic quest to take down the queen and avenge his traitorous father. No matter how tempting Ruby was, Lucas had to keep focused on his only purpose: keeping Elskov safe.

He smoothed his hair back into place. "You don't have to

protect me."

"Then who will?" Her jaw tightened and she blinked twice before jerking her chin down in a quick nod, all of the playfulness gone from her beautiful face. "Don't worry, I know it's not real, but we both have a mission here and it'll get done faster if we work together. Clock's ticking, remember?"

As if he could forget. He'd never wanted time to speed up and slow down at the same time so much before, but he had to pick. So he did. He grabbed the doorknob and pulled it open.

"And there they are," Ingrid exclaimed, rising from the table and walking toward them.

Ruby tucked her hand into the crook of his arm and they strode in together. Jasper and Clausen sat on one side of the long rectangle table flanked by Antoine and his entourage. On the other side of the table sat Rolf, Joey, a man who must be the minister, and Ingrid's empty chair. Formally dressed servants were busy going from one person to the next, pouring champagne into silver flutes.

"Congratulations, you've made it through the hand-binding and judging by the looks of you, all went well." Ingrid wiped her thumb against his jaw. "Lipstick," she whispered with a grin. "Now without further ado." She took a key out of her pocket and inserted it into the small lock holding the silver hand-binding chain around their wrists and then turned it. The chain fell away from their wrists. "Please take your seats at either end of the table and join us as we toast to your many happy years together."

Lucas rubbed the inside of his wrist. The chain hadn't been heavy or constricting, but being without it felt…weird. Glancing over, he saw Ruby doing the same as she made her way to the opposite end of the table. Once they sat down, everyone else stood and raised their glasses.

"To the happy couple," Rolf said, his smile not reaching all the way up to his eyes.

The champagne bubbles popped on Lucas's tongue as he sipped, keeping an eye on everyone else as they took their seats again.

"There is so much to do before the ceremony," Ingrid said as soon as she'd sat down in the chair to Lucas's left. "Take a good look at each other because you won't be seeing much of your bride-to-be until the minister pronounces you man and wife, especially not with you being relocated to Jasper's wing until then.

The fork bit into his palm and he forced himself to loosen his grip. "You're moving me?"

"Don't worry." She patted his forearm. "It's only for a few days, and then you'll be with your Ruby every day for the rest of your life."

The idea of that was far more tempting than it should be to a man who'd pledged his life and his loyalty to his country, especially when the woman in question was the daughter of one of Europe's most notorious crime bosses whom he just happened to have blackmailed into posing as his fiancée.

• • •

When the fifth straight pin jabbed her hip the next day, Ruby promised herself she'd never get married. No dress fittings. No seating arrangements. No bullshit. She bit down on her lip to stop from crying out when one of Antoine's minions stabbed her again when pinning the muslin dress pattern to fit her curves.

"Francine, you must be more careful," Antoine snarled as he circled the raised platform and apprised the lines of his creation, all of the sparkle in his eyes from the night before as he delivered several toasts in Ruby's and Lucas's honor replaced with the bloodshot eyes of the viciously hungover.

"I'm sorry," Francine said, her apology as real as the dark

circles under her blue eyes.

The whole team had worked overnight to get the dress to this stage and would pull even more all-nighters in their efforts to create a one-of-a-kind dress Ruby hoped like hell she'd never actually put on. Guilt pinched her conscience.

"It's okay," she said, giving Francine and the other members of Antoine's team a tired smile. "The compressed timeline isn't anyone's friend."

Her mother came up behind her and looked over her shoulder at the reflection of them both in the mirror. They wore matching resigned expressions.

"You look exhausted," Ingrid said.

"I didn't sleep well." Or at all. It was amazing how quickly she'd gotten used to having Lucas around constantly. She hadn't seen him since last night at dinner. Now they were only a few hours away from another family dinner sure to be filled with wedding questions she'd have to deflect or lie about.

After growing up on Fare Island, she would have thought herself immune to the stress of deception. She was wrong.

"It's only for a few days and then you'll have Luc by your side again." Ingrid squeezed her shoulders and then took a step back so Francine could pin the last few spots. "I know these traditions can seem silly in today's world, but it's the little things that keep us together."

Together. What was that? After all this was over, she'd be as alone as she'd ever been with her brother still acting as a double agent for the Americans, her mother trapped on the island as always, and Lucas doing whatever it took to keep Elskov safe. And her? What kind of life was there for a mobster's daughter after she left? She couldn't imagine a job where the ability to lie, steal, and manipulate were sought after skills.

• • •

Back in her own soft, pink dress no worse for wear, at least physically, from the dress fitting, Ruby stopped by the French doors leading out to the garden. The riot of color in the wildflower garden stretched as far as she could see. It was so very different from the structured garden at Moad Manor. Her heart sped up the moment she spotted him. In his severe black suit, Lucas should look out of place, but he didn't. He looked more at home out there surrounded by a sea of pink, blue, purple, red, and white. No matter where he was, Lucas always managed to make it his own without even trying. He'd certainly done so with her. He'd invaded her thoughts, breached her defenses, and made a place for himself.

She was out the door and crossing the flagstone patio before she had even thought about it. "Are you planning to interrogate the daisies?"

The dark brooding look disappeared as soon as he looked over at her and something clanked into place in her chest. No one ever looked at her like that—except for Lucas.

"They've been uncooperative," he said as he reached down and plucked off a bloom and tucked it in her hair, his fingers grazing the shell of her ear before trailing down the side of her throat.

Her heart raced and her mouth went dry. It had only been twenty-four hours since he'd last touched her in the shower, but it felt like forever.

Keep it together, Rubes. This is only a mission for him, and it may be your only way off this island. If Rolf finds out what you've been doing, you're dead before the thought even finishes processing.

It took almost every bit of self-control she had, but she managed not to reach out, not to respond, and not to react when the openness fled from his face, replaced by the stony reserve she recognized from when she'd arrived at Moad Manor. Her lungs grew tight, and she dug deep to keep her chin from trembling.

"Have you had any luck while I've been a human pincushion?" There, that sounded almost completely normal, if he missed the slight shake in the last few syllables, which he wouldn't. Lucas noticed everything.

His gaze narrowed, but he kept his hands clasped tightly behind his back. "I've been following Rolf all morning. That's why I'm out here. He's in his office." He jerked his chin toward the big bay window where Rolf stood with his back to the garden, oblivious to the spy in his midst. "I've yet to catch him alone, and the phone is always in his hand."

This whole thing would be so much easier if Rolf wasn't such a paranoid asshole. Of course, crime bosses who weren't didn't tend to last long.

"Is he with Joey?"

"No." Lucas shook his head and adjusted the daisy tucked behind her ear, but unlike before, his moves were efficient and cold, a cover, not an invitation—not that her body, desperate for his touch, recognized that. "Jasper and Clausen are trailing him. Last report stated he was on his way to the landing strip."

"So who is Rolf with?" She ducked away from his touch before she embarrassed herself and melted against him. Instead, she trailed her fingers across the hot-pink blooms while keeping the window in her peripheral vision.

"The Sparrow."

Her head shot up before she could get her reactions under control. "That's good."

Lucas grabbed her low on her waist and swung her around so her back was to the window and lowered his mouth so it was only a fraction of an inch away from her ear, no doubt for cover just in case her stepfather spotted them lingering in the garden outside his office. "How?"

Adrenaline and desire had her strung out and feeling like the only thing anchoring her to the earth was Lucas's hand on her hip. She inhaled a shaky breath and focused not on the vivid blue-green of his eyes but on the security and honesty he represented despite being the last man on earth she should trust.

"He may not be Rolf's second-in-command, but the Sparrow still knows everything that happens on Fare Island and a lot of what happens off of it." Her words came out in a rush. "We need to get to his cabin."

This could be it.

If the Sparrow still kept his paper notes tucked away under the false bottom of his desk drawer like he did when she was a kid, then they'd have all the information they needed to stop the arms deal and end this fake engagement. Slipping her hand into Lucas's and leading him through the hedgerow maze leading to the Sparrow's cabin should have been like taking the final exhilarating steps in a marathon. Instead, it felt like taking a running leap off one of the fjords and hoping like hell she wouldn't break apart on the rocks below.

• • •

Lucas did a double take. The Sparrow's cabin was located behind a green door secreted in the leafy wall of the hedgerow maze that opened to reveal a quiet courtyard with a small stone house in the middle. It looked so quiet and serene it set off every one of his warning sirens. Keeping one hand on the door handle and one wrapped around Ruby's arm to stop her from rushing forward, he scanned the perimeter and found... nothing. Not a single closed-circuit camera, guard dog, or security system.

Following Ruby inside the courtyard, he took a second look, trying to locate anything that either looked out of place or too perfect.

"You won't find it," Ruby said, smirking.

"What?"

"The surveillance equipment."

He may work for the good guys, but he wasn't one of them. Isn't that what the Sparrow and Jasper had been trying to warn her about? They were right, and when it came to thinking like the bad guys, no one was better at it than he was. He'd find whatever security the Sparrow had no matter what Ruby thought.

"Why's that?" he asked.

Her full lips turned that half smile into a full one that lit up her entire face. His girl loved giving him his comeuppance. "He doesn't have any."

That couldn't be right. He turned in a slow circle, taking in the high hedges, the manicured landscaping, and the stone cabin with its red door and cutesy flowerpots with bright yellow tulips. The whole place was bizarre, and he couldn't spot a telltale glimmer of surveillance anywhere.

"Why wouldn't he have surveillance?"

"Because he doesn't keep anything here that he doesn't care about anyone seeing." She gave him a conspiratorial wink. "Unless you know exactly where to look, which I do. Come on."

The inside of the cabin was as pin neat as the outside. There was a living-kitchen-dining room area that housed a bistro table, small desk, twin recliners, and a small television. There was a backdoor in the kitchen, giving them a second way out if necessary. He peeked through a door into a sparse bedroom featuring a twin bed and not a damn thing else. The only other door in the place led to a tiny bathroom.

Instead of stopping in front of the desk like he'd expected, Ruby walked over to the island dividing the kitchen area from the dining area. She moved the potted plant in the center of it to the counter and then ran her hand under the island's overhang.

"I thought any information would be in his desk." He

pointed toward the small desk with its orange cup of pens and stack of blank notepads.

She jerked her chin at the desk. "That's for show. This is the real thing." She tugged her bottom lip between her teeth and rolled her gaze up toward the ceiling in obvious concentration as her hands moved along the underside.

It shouldn't have turned him on, but there was so little about her that didn't. He adjusted his stance to accommodate his thickening cock as he tried and failed to stop memories of watching those lips swallow him up and the sharp prick of her teeth as she nibbled along the column of his throat. All of that was bad enough, but the real killer was the look of triumph that lit her beautiful face up from the curve of her bottom lip to the glimmer in her gray eyes that made her seem brighter than the rainbow highlights in her hair.

She beamed at him. "Got it."

There was a soft click, and the entire top of the island swung upward on silent hinges. Ruby did a little shimmy, hip-shaking dance move that sent all of the blood in his body rushing south.

Smart. Sexy. Fun as hell. If he were any other man, he would be dragging her off to the nearest bed, or figuring out how to sweet-talk her into making the wedding a real one. But he wasn't any other man, and there was no way the head of the Silver Knights could ever be with a crime boss's daughter, even if he was falling for her, hard. And that could be as effective as a double tap between the eyes. He couldn't afford to get distracted or have his loyalties divided, not if he was going to stop the exchange.

Shoving everything except that realization into a cold, dark hole, he strode to the secret desk and ignored the smell of her perfume, the tease of being so close to her, and the urge to get her the hell off this island and somewhere safe. They shuffled through the three neat stacks of papers in silence.

There were copies of shipping orders, dossiers on crime figures from across Northern Europe, and jotted down notes about deals. It was a fucking treasure trove of intel and not a damn thing about the deal with Henriksen.

"I don't like it." The Sparrow's voice came in through the cracked-open kitchen window.

He froze with sheaf of paper in his hand, the manifest for a shipment of black market antiquities, for half a heartbeat before training took over. Each sheet went back into place exactly where it had been before as the voices got closer. Sparing enough time to glance over at Ruby, he had his mouth half open to tell her what to do when he realized she was already doing it. She wasn't freaking out. She was putting everything back into position, quickly, and with the tight line of her lush mouth being the only giveaway that everything could blow up in their faces in about twenty seconds.

"You don't have to like it, you just have to do it." Rolf's voice. Closer, almost to the cabin. "You know what's at stake here."

The last piece of paper in place, he lowered the kitchen island's top. It clicked softly back into place. Ruby whipped around and grabbed the potted plant, placed it on the island, and adjusted it so it was in the same spot as before. Without a single word between them, they turned in unison and hustled silently to the backdoor.

"That bargaining chip won't always be in your possession." The Sparrow's voice was right outside the front door.

Lucas opened the backdoor. Ruby hurried through it with him on her heels. He was pulling it shut just as the front door began to open.

"The wedding changes nothing," Rolf said, his voice a low snarl. "Everyone knows it but you."

The closed backdoor blocked out whatever the Sparrow said in response. He rolled the conversation around in his head, examining the different possible meanings as he and Ruby slipped through a second gate cut into the hedges behind the Sparrow's cabin.

The wedding changes nothing.

A reference to the arms deal or something worse? He'd known he was putting Ruby in danger by blackmailing her into this plan, but that hadn't mattered before he'd met her. Now? It was like he'd swallowed a bag of glass shards.

Finally, far enough from the Sparrow's cabin to offer a modicum of safety, he wrapped his fingers around her wrist and pulled her to a stop beside him. His lips were on hers before his brain had caught up to his instinctual intention. She opened beneath him, wrapping her arms around his neck. It was an invitation he wasn't going to turn down. He swept his tongue inside, plundering her sweetness and teasing one of those soft moans from her.

The kiss wasn't a promise. It wasn't an apology. It was a wish he knew couldn't come true, but that didn't make him want her any less. There was more danger in that than all the goons on Fare Island.

A rustle up ahead sent adrenaline spiking through his veins, and he broke the kiss in time to see Ingrid come around the corner. He and Ruby jumped apart like kids caught making out in a school hallway.

"Oh, there you two are," Ingrid said, her eyes less focused and duller than usual, the air of manic energy replaced by an almost drowsy haze. "Come on, Ruby darling, you need to help with the seating arrangements. Nearly everyone has said yes, and I think Rolf invited half of Europe, and you know most of them hate each other, which is going to make dinner an unholy misery."

Giving him a wan smile, she linked her arm through Ruby's and led her back to the main house while all Lucas could do was watch from a distance as she disappeared inside.

Chapter Eleven

The next night, after another day of fake wedding preparation madness and frustrated attempts to steal some alone time with Lucas to search for any information about the arms exchange, Ruby cut into her lamb chop and tried to focus on her mother's question about the wedding bouquet.

"She doesn't give a damn, Ingrid," Rolf slurred from behind a full plate and a nearly empty glass at the head of the dinner table. "Just do what you want."

It might be true, but it didn't change the fact that her stepfather was drunk and an asshole. Since he was a total prick when he was sober, Ruby had a lifetime of practice dealing with that aspect of his personality. The slurred words and bitter snarl right on the surface instead of under a thin veneer of smarm was new, though.

There hadn't been a lot of non-Ingrid-wedding chatter at the dinner table up to that point, but the room went silent at his comment. Across the table from her and Lucas, Jasper and Talia went still, their forced cheer and false flirting quashed by the tension. Lucas tucked her hand into his under the table, and her shoulders ratcheted down from her earlobes at his warm, comforting touch.

"Are you feeling all right, dear?" Ingrid asked in a small voice from her spot at the opposite end of the table from her husband.

"Why wouldn't I be? I'm sitting here surrounded by those who love me most." He shot back the rest of the akvavit in his glass. "I'm a man who has it all, aren't I, darling?"

He added enough derision into what should have been an endearment to force an angry heat up from Ruby's toes fast enough she was surprised her hair didn't catch fire. Lucas's cool grip on her hand was the only thing keeping her grounded in the moment rather than flying across the table and letting the bastard have it, once and for all.

Her mom smiled, but it was a small one that didn't even come close to reaching her eyes. "Of course."

"Excellent answer." He reached for the decanter next to his glass. "Shall we have a toast to the happy couple?"

Ruby stiffened at the words that came out of her stepfather's mouth that sounded six shades of ugly. "I don't think that's necessary."

The engagement may be a cover, but her stepfather didn't know that. She glanced down at her fingers intertwined with Lucas's. His words stung all the more because she was beginning to wish it wasn't all a lie, that she really was about to have life beyond the borders of Fare Island and outside of her stepfather's criminal organization.

"You've never been as agreeable as your mother, have you?" Rolf asked, pouring a double's worth of liquor into his glass. "Why is that? Have I not given you everything you could want?" He toyed with his glass so that the ice cubes swirled around inside, just one more thing he sent this way or that, depending on his mood. "If it wasn't for me, God knows what would have happened to the little trio. No doubt your mother would be in ja—"

"Rolf. That's enough." Ingrid's voice was as sharp and as mean as one of the Sparrow's deadly blades. "May I speak with you outside?"

She pushed her chair away from the table with a loud screech and stood, her white-knuckled hands in fists at her side.

"Anything for you, darling. You know that." Rolf's chair stuttered as it went back, little jerks that made the ice in his glass clink hard against each other, then stood and walked with deliberate intention to the door and swung it open with more force than necessary. "Shall we?"

Heels clicking on the hardwood floor, Ingrid crossed the room with an extra bit of iron in her spine that Ruby couldn't recall ever seeing before. First, Jasper and his secret life working with the Americans, and now her mom standing up to Rolf. Maybe Jasper was right. Maybe they didn't need her to always be watching out for them, running interference, and cleaning up their—mostly Jasper's—messes. If that was the case, she had no idea what to do next. Keeping them safe had been the only thing she'd ever really worried about.

"After you, my lady." Rolf executed a mocking bow.

Ignoring him, Ingrid looked back at the rest of them. "Please don't wait on us to continue with your dessert."

After that she swept through the door. Rolf closed it behind both of them.

Lucas let go of her hand. "Thank God. I didn't think Osborne's latest invention was going to work."

"Was it the alcohol volume doubler?" Talia asked, pulling a gold tube of lipstick and a small gold compact out of her bra.

"Yes. The man is a giant pain in my ass, but he's a genius." Lucas vaulted up from his seat and made a beeline toward Rolf's vacant seat.

Lucas, Jasper, and Talia moved in concert to her

stepfather's empty spot at the head of the table while Ruby sat frozen in her seat trying to process what in the hell was going on. While she'd been stuck looking at menus and seating charts, her brother, his fake girlfriend, and Lucas had been up to something much more interesting. This was bullshit. Her ass was on the line as much as theirs, if not more, and yet they left her in the dark.

"Watch the door," Lucas said as he picked up Rolf's phone.

Jasper snorted. "You watch the fucking door."

"I'm point," Lucas shot back. "You're just the interfering brother."

"Who is working with the Americans," Jasper grumbled as he stalked to the door.

Talia uncapped the lipstick, revealing a USB drive instead of the pale-pink shade she wore on her lips. She handed it to Lucas along with her matching compact mirror.

"How long?" He slipped off the back of Rolf's phone and then pushed the compact's decorative hinge to reveal a plug that he fit into the phone's exposed inner-workings.

"Forty-five seconds," Talia said.

After a quick beep, he flipped the clasp that held the compact closed and slipped the lipstick USB into it. "In the lab or real world?"

"This device has never been used on the job before," she said.

"And you thought this was the ideal time to field test a new toy?" He cut a glare at the other Silver Knight.

Talia didn't flinch. The woman had to be made of solid ice. "Osborne guaranteed it would download the virus that would let us monitor the phone remotely, no matter what encryption is on it."

"It won't be his dead ass getting dumped in the North Sea if he's wrong." Lucas dropped his gaze back to the compact, the mirror showing a countdown clock instead of a reflection.

"He never is."

The whole thing was like having a front row seat to a spy movie, but it wasn't enough. She wanted—needed—to be a part of it.

"Twenty seconds." Lucas glanced up at the door. "Can you hear them?"

"Voices are low, but they're going at it." Jasper's jaw was clenched hard enough to break a tooth.

It wasn't like they hadn't heard Rolf in all his nasty glory before, but their mother wasn't usually the target. No. It was his stepchildren who had grown up dealing with the verbal shanks. Both of them had learned how to zone out as he sliced and diced them. Their mother hadn't. Despite her unusual show of spirit tonight, Rolf's barbs had to be hitting their mark if Jasper's reaction was anything to go by.

"Ten seconds," Lucas announced in a hushed voice.

Jasper stiffened. "They stopped."

The doorknob turned.

"We need five more seconds," Lucas said.

Jasper grabbed the knob and held it still before shoving his shoulder against the door.

"Three seconds." The vein in Lucas's temple throbbed.

Ruby's heart clogged her throat.

"What is going on with this door?" Jasper mumbled loudly, sounding almost as drunk as Rolf. "It won't open."

"Done." Lucas unplugged Rolf's phone from the compact converter and tossed it to Talia before setting the phone back down where it had been next to the decanter.

He hustled back over to his chair and sat down a moment before Jasper released the door.

Ingrid stood by herself on the other side, hands on her hips and a weary downturn to her mouth. Ruby tried to hyperventilate as quietly as possible while Lucas took a bite of the creamy Skyr panna cotta with raspberries and licorice shavings as if it was just another boring family dinner.

"Did you forget how a door worked, Jasper?" Ingrid asked, her tone softer than her words, before strolling into the room and heading straight to Rolf's seat. "Ah, there it is. Your father refused to retire to his room until he had this damn thing. I'm going to deliver it." She picked up the phone in one hand and rubbed her temple with the other. "After that we really need to finalize the dinner menu, Ruby. Do you mind coming up to my rooms so we can do that? I'm afraid my head is really beginning to ache."

"Of course." She stood up, playing the ever dutiful daughter while mentally plotting how to get Lucas alone and make it known she wasn't sitting on the sidelines again. "Good night everyone."

She brushed a kiss against Lucas's cheek to cover what she had to do next. "Tomorrow. Noon. The library."

How she'd sneak away from all of the fake wedding plans she was sure her mom had, she didn't know, but she would. No matter how hot he was, her Silver Knight wasn't going to keep her clueless again.

· · ·

The next afternoon, Lucas had to pass by Rolf's office on his way to the library. Taking a quick peek in, the first thing he spotted was Joey glowering in a corner; the second was a green-faced Rolf hurtling straight at him. The older man's shoulder slammed into Lucas's, sending both men backpedaling to regain their balance. Lucas came back, hands loose at his sides but primed to strike. One close look at Rolf, though, and he changed his mind. Landing a solid hit would probably result in his shoes swimming in puke.

Rolf steadied himself with a hand on the doorframe.

"Luc."

"Are you okay?" he asked, taking a safety step back.

The older man shook his head then groaned, obviously regretting the movement. "Not feeling well."

Lucas gave him a once over. Bloodshot eyes. Green pallor. Dry, cracked lips. Rolf was hungover hard. Osborne would be eager to hear about the alcohol doubler's after effects, but Lucas had no interest in being on the receiving end of them.

He pivoted out of Rolf's way. "I won't hold you up then."

The other man narrowed his eyes, distrust written all over his face underneath the obvious signs of the mother of all hangovers. "What are you doing down here?"

"Ruby asked me to meet her in the library." Lies of omission were always better than straight-up falsehoods, especially when dealing with a dangerous man like Rolf who would only be more suspicious and on edge when injured. "I think she needed a break from wedding planning."

And to chew his ass up one side and down the other for last night. He hadn't missed the annoyance in her voice when she'd issued her edict before she'd strutted out of the dining room last night. Someone didn't like being left out of things. After growing up in a place like Fare Island, he could understand how not being in the know led to bad things — like one of the Sparrow's blades in your back.

Rolf looked like he was about to say something else, but clamped his mouth shut tight, shuddered, turned another shade of green, and then took off at a fast clip for the stairs.

Now that was a man he didn't envy.

Shaking his head, he turned his attention back to the office. Joey stood inside the doorway, his beefy arms crossed over his chest and a scowl curling up one lip. Obviously, the Macintosh crime syndicate's number two man thought he was a badass. He was wrong.

Lucas cocked his head and grinned at the muscle-bound

idiot. "It's really too bad your mother never warned you that your face would freeze like that."

Not waiting for the oaf's reaction when he finally managed to untangle the insult, Lucas continued down the hallway to the library two doors farther down.

The double doors were open. Ruby stood with her back to him on the opposite side of the room in front of a pair of French doors that looked out onto the gardens. It reminded him of the first day he'd met her at Moad Manor when she'd taken one look at the flowers behind the house and noticed more about them than he had in three months of living there. He'd been ready for the woman he'd thought Ruby was, he hadn't been prepared for the woman she'd turned out to be.

He closed the door behind him. She turned at the quiet click of the door shutting, her pale-pink skirt fluttering around her knees and giving him the perfect view of her long legs that had felt so damn good wrapped around him. Ruby cleared her throat, dragging his attention to her face, framed by her wild rainbow hair, and didn't hide her amusement at his distraction.

"This is all very cloak-and-dagger," he said, walking toward her, as if he could even pretend to stay away.

"It should be right up your alley, then." She played with the long gold chain around her neck, the length of which disappeared beneath the low V of her white shirt. "You should have let me know about what was going on last night."

Her technique was basic spy tradecraft. A quick diversion followed by a direct strike with the intention of getting your target to share crucial information before they'd realized what he or she was saying. No doubt the intel game came easy to her, but he wasn't the kind of mark she was used to when sent out on errands by her stepfather.

Letting his gaze wander over her every curve, his fingers twitching to touch even the smallest sliver of exposed skin, he crossed to her. "Was it that easy for you with the men Rolf targeted to rob of their prize jewels? A little push. A little peek. Then he'd hand over his passwords?"

She didn't back away. Instead, she took a step closer so their bodies were only a few inches apart, electricity sparking between them like a transformer on overload. "Pretty close."

"Did you like it?" Again, his focus dropped to her perfect mouth as he imagined all the things he wanted her to do with it.

As if she knew exactly what he was thinking because she was too, the tip of her pink tongue darted out and wet her lush lips. "The thrill of the adrenaline rush? Yes. The knowing that any man who met me was destined to be either much poorer or dead afterward? Not so much." Her chin trembled and she closed her eyes for a split second before opening them again and staring up at him with renewed intensity. "Now answer my question. Why not bring me into your little circle of trust with Jasper and Talia?"

A sense that he'd used her too much already? A worry that he wouldn't be able to keep her safe once he was gone? A fear that the more time he spent with her, the more likely he was to forget the real reason he was on Fare Island? All true, and none of which he could say.

A lie of omission is always better than a straight-up falsehood.

"You're not an agent," he said.

She rolled her eyes. "No, but my dead body will be sinking to the bottom of the North Atlantic right along with yours if something goes wrong."

"Nothing will go wrong."

"You can't promise that."

"Never doubt my word." He'd do what it took. He'd find a way. He wouldn't leave her swinging between life and death because he'd blackmailed her in to helping him.

"I'm not going to sit back and be only an observer. I'm in this as deep as you are."

If she were anyone else, he'd be recruiting her to be part of the Silver Knights and sweet-talking her back into his bed as soon as they got to Elskov. She was as brave as she was ferociously determined, and he already knew how deep her loyalties were for those she cared about. But the fact was, she wasn't anyone else. She was Ruby Macintosh, daughter of one of North Europe's most powerful crime bosses. There was no future for them, in or out of his bed. He couldn't give her the freedom she deserved or the job she'd be fucking fantastic at, but he could make her a part of this operation.

"Fair enough, not that we've gotten anything out of last night's work." A fact that made his head pound almost as hard as Rolf's must be. "Your stepfather isn't using his phone."

Ruby laughed. "Yeah, I saw him going into his office earlier. I almost felt bad for him."

"He's probably throwing up his guts in his room now." Next time he'd half the dosage. "Only Joey's left in the office."

"Not for long." She gave him an ornery grin that promised trouble ahead.

"Why do you say that?"

"Because you forget that I know this place better than you do. There's more to me than colorful hair and an invitation to Fare Island."

"Okay, so what do you know?"

"That Joey has never missed a meal in his life. Ever." She strutted to the door and dropped her hand to the knob. "And that's not going to change today when its Thursday, and that means his favorite meatballs, rye bread, and pickled gherkins."

Because of the general pre-wedding chaos, the cook had made a full lunch that a couple of servants had set out on a side table. It was up to each house resident to serve themselves. No one would be bringing a tray to Joey, forcing him to abandon Rolf's office for the dining room.

"How did you know Rolf wouldn't be up for an evening in the office?" he asked as he walked over to stand beside her.

"He's not a big drinker. Chances were slim to none that he'd be as happy as spring sheep today."

She held her finger up to her lip and peeked around the library's open door. Lucas had to shift so he stood behind her in order to see. That brought his body in line with hers in a way that made his cock wake up and say hello. With the perfect timing of an executioner, Joey strolled out of Rolf's office and down the hall toward the dining room. As tempting as it was to stay pressed against her, they couldn't miss this opportunity. They were out the door as soon as Joey turned the corner.

The office was empty. Shutting the door after Ruby ducked inside, Lucas made a beeline for Rolf's desk. There were papers everywhere but no calendar. Working in unison without uttering a word, they searched through the stacks for any tidbit about Henriksen, a shipment of guns, or the exchange location, coming up empty on all counts.

Ten minutes later, they stood side by side staring at the desk making sure everything was in the same order as it had been before. Frustration was turning his gut into a seething pool of destructive acid, but he turned the business card for a shady art dealer a fraction of an inch to the left to its original position. This whole operation was turning into a bust and time was running out. They had days, not weeks, before Henriksen got ahold of the weapons and launched his guerrilla campaign on Elskov.

"Maybe the books?" Ruby asked, surveying the bookshelf behind the desk. "He's not much of a reader, and I always wondered if he kept the books for another reason."

Thick, leather-bound hardcover volumes with titles like *An Academic Deconstruction of Viking Lore* and *The Great*

Fjord Battles of 835 ran the length of the bookshelf. None looked like anything that Rolf would sit down with next to a crackling blaze in the fireplace.

He was reaching for the closest book when he heard footsteps. Reaching for Ruby, he looked over his shoulder at the closed office door. The knob turned. Grabbing her wrists in one hand, he lifted her arms above her head as he maneuvered her so her back was up against the bookshelves, her legs parted enough that he could step between them.

The door squeaked open.

"Luc—"

He cut off her question with a kiss. She parted her mouth in surprise. Taking advantage of the moment to delve deeper wasn't something that should happen. It did anyway. When it came to Ruby, things had a way of working out that way.

Dropping his free hand to her hip and sneaking his thumb under the hem of her shirt to stroke her bare skin underneath at the same time as he slid his tongue inside her sweet mouth, he reveled in the feel of her smooth skin and the taste of her delicious kiss. The truth of it was, Ruby wasn't an asset, she wasn't a pawn in this operation. She was the woman he never thought he'd find—the one he didn't want to be without.

"What in the hell are you two doing in here?" Joey yelled.

Lucas tore his mouth away from Ruby's and lowered her arms to her sides but couldn't seem to let go of her. Holding onto her hand, he turned to face Rolf's snarling second-in-command.

The other man stood in the doorway, his right hand on the gun butt sticking out of his shoulder holster and his left held a plate heaped high with meatballs and bread.

"What's it look like?" Ruby asked, her voice convincingly breathy. "Hiding from mom."

Looking from one of them the other, Joey slowly moved his hand away from his gun to get a better grip on his overfilled plate. "This room is off-limits. Get out."

"Fine." Ruby tossed her head, the sun steaming in from one of the windows making the brightly colored hues sparkle like a real rainbow. "No one wants to be here now that you're here anyway."

With that she flounced to the door, all attitude and snobbery. Damn. His girl was cool under pressure, even if her strut seemed a little on the shaky side as she passed by Joey and went out into the hall.

Lucas took a slower route, taking his time as he crossed the room like he owned it. Sure, it was an asshole move, but he was okay with that. Sometimes being a dick was the only way to get the message across, and he did have one for Joey: Ruby was off-limits. Now. Tomorrow. When Lucas was no more than a memory. Joey might see her as a way to ensure he'd eventually be number one in the Macintosh organization, but that wasn't going to happen.

Accidentally knocking into the other man's shoulder as he passed, Lucas kept his gaze straight ahead and didn't slow down as he walked out of the office.

"My mom went into the dining room." Ruby grabbed his hand and pulled him in the opposite direction. "We're going to the kitchen."

The kitchen was behind the wide staircase leading to the second floor. Open and airy, it was the domain of the single cook and her handful of minions—all of whom were on the staff patio enjoying their lunch in the sunshine.

"That was close." A pink flush brightened Ruby's cheeks as she opened the cabinet next to the sink that held the water glasses.

"And still no answers." That was the nut of it. He couldn't keep playing fake fiancé, no matter how much he and his cock liked it. "Time is running out and we're like a cow on ice trying to stay upright."

Ruby let out a surprised gasp and peeked around the open cabinet door at him, her eyes wide with glee. "Time to get back to dry land then." She pushed the cabinet door open wide so he could see what was hanging on the inside. "My mom's calendar."

A peel and stick dry erase calendar took up the bottom half of the door. The notes on the calendar had a feminine turn to them and listed things such as florist numbers, a few wedding details, and a listing underneath the Sunday heading that read:

R. FLIGHT ARRIVES 10 A.M. SUNDAY, LE GRAND DUCAL HOTEL, LUXEMBOURG

"That's it," Lucas said, shaking his head in disbelief. "It's been out in the open all along."

Adrenaline rushed through his veins as a plan started to form. He'd let the team know. They'd alert Interpol. Agents would be routed to Luxembourg.

"So what happens now?" Ruby asked as she softly closed the cabinet, keeping her face averted from him.

"My room's bugged." It wasn't, but something wouldn't let him leave her yet, not when he could hear the clock ticking down in his head. "Let's go to yours. I need to make a call and then we need to call off the wedding."

The words tasted foul on his tongue, but he couldn't think about that now. He had a country to save, and whether he lost part of himself in the process shouldn't matter.

Chapter Twelve

Ruby sat on the edge of her bed and watched Lucas as he talked to someone on his team about available agents and Interpol. It was fascinating to see him like this, in all of his master-of-his-domain glory as he prowled her room issuing orders and plotting Henriksen's downfall.

The whole show was turning her on. Chewing on her bottom lip in a failed effort to distract herself from noticing the way his suit pants fit perfectly on his tight ass and the way his mussed hair and the determined line of his jaw gave him an air of hot badassery, she exhaled a deep breath. The action only emphasized the way the lace of her bra scraped against her sensitive nipples.

"So we'll set up Gundersen as a hotel employee and Aster as a guest," Lucas said, rubbing his palm hard across the back of his hair, making it stand on end. "Berg and Pedersen should set up outside the hotel in twelve-hour shifts."

He nodded several times, uttering a few nonsensical acronyms that must have made sense to the person on the other end of the line before hanging up and slipping the phone back into his pocket.

"So what happens now?" she asked, not sure she wanted to hear the answer.

"We call off the wedding and get you the hell off this island."

She could disappear and start over. Jasper didn't need her looking over his shoulder any more. He had the entire American government doing that. Having a permanent spy in the Macintosh organization was too valuable to let anything happen to him. Her mom had finally found her backbone, how much longer before she walked away from Fare Island? What if the only thing tying her here were her kids? If they left, would she too?

It seemed like Ruby's world was full of breathless possibilities instead of well-loved burdens, but when she tried to imagine where she could go, the only thing that popped to mind was a garden of lavender, comfortable chairs perfect for reading in the sun, and a dark-haired, blue-eyed man coming out of the manor house, heading straight for her.

And that was never going to happen.

Her throat ached, but she forced the words out anyway with a bravado she didn't feel. "So I guess this is good-bye."

The muscles in his shoulders went tight, and his eyes darkened dangerously. "I don't want it to be."

"That makes two of us, but it doesn't change facts." She lifted her chin and dredged up any bit of self-control she had not to bound up from the bed and run straight into his arms. "I'm not the kind of girl who ends up with the good guy. I'm the crime boss's daughter."

"That's where you're wrong." He stalked over to her, every step an act of aggression no doubt meant to intimidate her and push his message home. "The Sparrow and your bother, they know the score. I did terrible things before I joined the Silver Knights. Luc Svendsen, and all his misdeeds, isn't just a cover. It's my real name. It's who I really am. Every blackmail scheme, every extortion, all of the lives ruined, and dishonest schemes enabled, I did that. If Dominick Rasmussen hadn't seen a use for me and recruited me into the resistance when Henriksen's father was still riding high on the success of his coup to overthrow the Elskovian monarchy, given me a new last name and a purpose, I'd still be selling secrets to the highest bidder. I'm not a good guy."

He loomed over her, a massive, uncompromising brick wall of wrong. If he expected her to back down, he was seriously mistaken.

"Bullshit." She stood up from the bed, forcing him to take a step back to make room for her. "Who you used to be isn't important, it's who you are now that counts."

Crossing his arms, he gave her a hard look. "Always such a tough chick with all the answers."

"Coming from you…" She shot him a sassy smirk. "I take that as a compliment."

"It is." A grin tugged one corner of his mouth.

"We aren't going to get all soft and mushy now, are we?"

"You always seem to have the opposite effect on me."

Her gaze dropped to where his hard cock pushed against the confines of his pants. Her mouth went dry. If this was the last time she got to see Lucas, she sure as hell was going to see all of him.

"Do I make you horny?" she asked in her best silly British spy impersonation, needing to put some emotional distance between them before she just gave in and admitted what she already knew was true.

She wasn't just falling for him—she already had.

He cupped the side of her face with his hand and dragged his thumb across her bottom lip, staring at her with a look of such focused intensity in his eyes that she was surprised she didn't spontaneously combust on the spot.

"That's not a good enough word to describe what you do to me," he said, his voice a low rumble that was made of equal parts awe and frustration. "You distract me from the rest of the world. You make me lose my ability to think about anything else, but how good you feel in my arms. You tempt me just by breathing. Believe me, I love everything you can do to me with that mouth of yours, but it's what comes out of it that lets me know I'll never find anyone else like you."

She gulped. "I thought you didn't like my smart mouth."

"I like it *too* much." His hand dropped to the hem of her shirt, but he didn't make a move to inch it up. Instead he teased her with the weight of his fingers against her.

"Stop talking." It came out more like a desperate plea than demand.

Lucas dipped his head but stopped short of her lips. "But there's more to say."

No. She couldn't take any more. Walking away from him was going to be hard enough without more words like those to replay on an endless loop in her head. "Shut up and kiss me."

• • •

The desperate, needy edge in her voice tore away the last shreds of control Lucas had been holding onto because, despite what she'd argued, he wasn't a good guy. A better man would have found a way to walk away. He may not be that man, but he could be her man tonight. So he did what she asked—what they both wanted—and kissed her.

Soft, pouty lips. Sweet, hungry mouth. Sexy little moan. It was as familiar and exhilarating as watching the sunrise after a nightlong storm, the kind that made the single-pane windows in the cheap apartment he'd grown up in rattle like they'd shatter at any moment. He could experience this kiss a million times, and each time would be as thrilling as the first. She parted her lips, and he deepened the kiss, plunging inside and claiming her as if he had the right to. Touching her was bliss and agony and something he'd never even dreamed about, but it wasn't enough. He needed all of her.

Never breaking their connection, he wrapped an arm around her waist and tugged her down with him as he dropped to the bed so she landed astride him. He threaded the fingers of one hand into her thick hair, pulling her closer even though there wasn't a centimeter of sunlight that could have gotten between them at the moment.

She undulated against him, rubbing her damp core against his hard cock. Pleasure streaked through his body, making him as hard as she was soft. It would have been heaven if it weren't for all the clothing between him and her silky skin.

Breaking the kiss, he trailed his lips across her jaw until he got to that soft spot behind her ear that made her entire body tremble. "Damn, I love it when you do that."

"Makes two of us," she said in a languorous purr as she turned her head enough for him to get a better angle.

He sucked her earlobe, raking his teeth across the sensitive flesh as he did so and grabbed her skirt-covered ass in his hands, holding her hard against him as she rocked her hips.

"Fuck me," he gasped, the rest of the world obliterated by the sensation threatening to overwhelm him.

She had the audacity to chuckle. "Yes please."

Smart mouth. Oh yes, she had one, and it made him hard as fucking concrete. But if she still had enough thinking power to make smart-ass remarks, then he wasn't getting the job done. He dragged his hands up from the full globes of her ass to her waist, and before she had a chance to realize his intent, flipped her onto her back, and then he got up from the bed.

The sight knocked him stupid. There she was on the bed

with her kiss-swollen lips, wild rainbow-colored hair spread out over the duvet, and her skirt hiked up to mid-thigh showing off her mouth-watering long legs, and he forgot his own name.

"Are you just going to look?" she teased, tugging her skirt high enough that he got a good view of the bright-blue silk panties covering his favorite place in the known universe.

God, she was killing him, and he'd never been so happy about the possibility of death. "Your clothes have got to go."

One eyebrow shot up. "Only mine?"

"Such a smart mouth." He took out his wallet, pulled a condom out of it, and tossed it onto the bedside table.

"And you love it." She shimmied out of her skirt and made quick work of whipping off her shirt.

Love. Ruby. His fingers flubbed on his shirt's first button as the truth slammed through him like a steel battering ram against a wall of dried-out twigs. As asinine as it was, he'd gone and done the one thing he swore to himself he would never do, especially not with her. He'd fallen for the girl he could never have. Before he could say anything, even if he'd had the vocabulary to do so, she rose up on her knees on the bed and went to work on his belt.

. . .

Ruby ached with need, every nerve ending tingling and desperate for Lucas's touch. Her core clenched as she lowered the zipper of his pants, slow enough to elicit a tortured groan from him. Good. This was how she wanted him, as lost in desire as she was.

Finally, when she couldn't stand to wait any longer, she pushed his pants down and took the long, thick length of him in her hand. Pressing her thumb against the sensitive spot right under the head, she leaned forward and lapped up the glistening drop of pre-come on the swollen tip. She looked up at him as she slowly slid her tongue over her lips, spreading that first taste of him.

"Ruby."

God, she loved the sound of her name coming from his mouth. Instead of answering, though, she went back to his cock, taking him inside her mouth and curling her tongue around his width as she sucked him deeper. Tasting him, stroking him with her tongue. Taking him as far as she could, even with one hand wrapped around the base of him and the other cupping his balls.

It shouldn't be this good. He wasn't even touching her. Still, she was slick with desire, and the demanding ache she'd had a few moments ago had grown to an undeniable need. She sat back and let him slip from her mouth.

"I need you," she said, stroking her hand up and down his now wet shaft before giving it a quick kiss.

"Lucky for you." He kicked off his shoes and took off his pants and underwear in one downward sweep. He reached behind his neck and tugged his shirt over his head, not even bothering to unbutton it all the way. "I'm here to serve."

Thank God for big favors.

"Lie back on the bed."

It wasn't a request, it was an order delivered in a rough timbre that made her nipples pucker—and judging by the bad-boy smirk on his face, he knew exactly the effect he was having on her. Not doing it wasn't an option she even wanted to consider. Of course, that didn't mean she wasn't going to give him a little bit of sass back.

She sat back on her heels then tugged her bottom lip between her teeth, reached behind her back, and unhooked her bra.

His cock jerked in response to her teasing act of defiance. "You're not following orders."

"I'm a very bad girl that way." She folded one arm across her chest to hold the lace in place and then slipped one bra strap off and then switching, doing the same with the other.

A muscle in Lucas's cheek twitched as he watched, silent and intense, but otherwise, he didn't move.

She lowered her arm. The bra followed. Keeping her gaze locked on his face, she licked the tips of her thumb and first finger then used them to pinch her already hard nipples, rolling them and pulling them taut.

His hands fisted, but he remained still.

"Oh, you'll give me nothing until I lie down, huh?" she asked. "Whatever will I do?"

She released her nipple and slid her fingers lightly down her stomach to the top of her panties. Raising herself up on her knees, she slipped her fingers under the waistband and between her wet folds. Even though the lace covered her, it was see-through enough for him to have a partially-obstructed view of her fingers circling her clit in unhurried strokes. She was so turned on that it wouldn't take long, but she wanted to come with him so she stopped and lifted her slick fingers to his mouth.

"Taste," she said.

The word hung in the air between them.

"I will," he practically growled. "But not like that."

He moved so fast she didn't see it coming, grabbing her behind the knees and yanking so she flopped onto her back. Half a second later, her panties were sailing through the air to land somewhere on the clothing-littered floor and her legs were spread wide. She figured he would dive in without any hesitation. She was wrong.

Taking his time, he kissed, nipped, and licked his way down the inside of her leg, his grip an iron vise not letting her pull away when he hit a tickle spot or one so sensitive that her hips came off the bed, her clit vibrating in response.

"No escaping now," he said. "You started this. It's only finished when you come so hard you forget your own name."

The comeback on the tip of her tongue evaporated the moment his tongue touched her in firm, unhurried licks so good they bordered on torture. The feel. The sound. The electric pulses jolting through her. They were as overwhelming as they were welcome. He lowered one leg to the bed, pushing it out as far as it would go, and began to stroke her folds, spreading her wide so she was utterly and completely open to him.

The vulnerability of it crept into her head, scaring her and tugging her away from the pleasure.

"It's okay," he murmured against her. "I've got you."

And he did. She knew it the same way she knew the northern lights would send streaks of green across the sky in the fall—and tonight she'd pretend it could be that way forever. She pushed away the fear and relaxed.

"That's it." He lapped at her clit and plunged first one and then another finger into her, curling them so he rubbed against her G-spot. "So tight." Another lick. "So good." He twisted his fingers, stroking them in and out in a steady rhythm. "So perfect."

The vibrations started in her thighs, ebbing and flowing like waves that crashed into each other.

"Lucas." She could barely get his name out, it was too much.

"Let it come, I've got you."

He sucked her clit into his mouth while pressing his tongue hard against its base, relenting and repeating it over and over again as the sensations increased and took her higher and higher until her orgasm broke her into a million pieces. And like he promised, Lucas was there for her as she came down back into herself, slowly, breath by breath. When she could focus again, there he was, wrapped around her and holding her close. His fingers traced the line of her hip and outer thigh, getting as far as her knee before making the feather-light journey back up.

A deeper desire took hold of her, one that didn't call for an explosion outward so much as the aching need to be filled, to be completed. "I might still remember my name."

His quiet laugh and increased pressure of his hard cock nestled against her ass were his only responses.

She rotated her hips, relishing the feel of him against her but needing to feel more. "You've made me greedy."

"For what?" He reached around and cupped her breast, rubbing his thumb against her nipple.

Her breath caught. "You."

He rolled her nipple until it peaked. "That I can give you."

"Tonight." There was something masochistic about her insistence on reminding herself of the temporary nature of this, but she needed to, because tomorrow was going to hurt enough without the little white lies meant to comfort that only delayed the inevitable heartbreak.

"Ruby, we—"

"Have only tonight." She rolled so she faced him, pushed him onto his back, and grabbed the condom from the bedside table. "Let's make the most of it."

• • •

Already on the edge after watching her come, Lucas held his breath as Ruby rolled the condom onto his straining cock. That was bad enough. When she lowered herself down onto him, so tight, he had to do equations to keep from losing it right there. He clamped his hands onto her hips and held her still against him, loving that he had the taste of her on his lips even as his dick was buried in her.

"This is more than tonight." It had to be. Something this

right didn't disappear when the sun came up.

She didn't argue. She didn't agree. Instead, she tossed back her head, planted her palms on his chest, and rode him hard, grinding her clit against his pelvic bone at the end of each downward stroke. It was almost enough to drive them both into oblivion, but he wasn't going as a passive observer. Hell no.

He took one hand off her hips and wrapped her long hair around his fist, pulling her head back. She made that moan that just about killed him every time and increased her pace, arching her back even more. The angle allowed him to hit the sensitive nerves just inside her entrance with each forward and retreat. It was beyond good, but he needed to feel her come all over him. He released her hip and reached between them so he could circle her clit with his thumb. She tightened around him and he nearly lost it. Keeping an iron grip on the last shreds of his self-control, he kept himself right on the edge, refusing to fall into the abyss until she did.

Her legs began to shake and she rocked harder against him, digging her nails into his chest. One. Two. Three strokes. She came with a harsh groan, squeezing him tight.

Only then did he follow her over, raising his hips off the bed and driving into her as deep as he could. Five rough, deep strokes and his balls tightened. The vibrations built at the base of his spine, and he made one final thrust before coming hard enough level a brick wall.

Ruby collapsed next to him, her chest heaving in time with his own. He closed his eyes and tried to catch his breath. At least that was what he tried to tell himself. The truth was, he didn't want to let her go. It was idiotic. It was illogical. It was fact.

"I'll be right back," he said before taking a quick trip to the bathroom to discard the condom and then turn off the bedroom lights.

When he got back, she was curled up on her side. He got into bed beside her, pulling the covers over both of them, and tucked her in close to him. He stroked her hair, so smooth and cool, as she snuggled closer. With any other woman this was the moment when he snuck out, but there was nowhere he'd rather be than with the woman he loved, even if it was only until dawn.

"Love you, rainbow girl," he whispered against her hair, the words coming from a place in him that he didn't even know existed until he met her.

She propped her chin up on his chest, the look in her eyes as sad as it was wistful. "I wish it was a simple as that."

He wasn't a man for games or fantasies. Life had taught him long ago how stupid it was to lie to yourself, but he couldn't help himself. For as long as he could make the night last, he'd do what he always seemed to do when it came to Ruby—he'd break his own rules because being with her was worth it.

"For tonight, let's pretend it's that simple." He pushed a strand of blue hair away from her face.

"I love you," she said, then brushed a kiss across his lips and laid her head down in the pocket of his shoulder.

What else was there to say? They couldn't make plans for the future. They couldn't commiserate about the past. They only had right now. So he held her close as she drifted off to sleep, but he couldn't.

There was too much he wanted to memorize about her, the slope of her shoulder, the line of her neck, the curve of her hip, the feel of her fitted perfectly against him like she'd been made just for him. It was one of his life's cruelest ironies that the only woman he'd even fallen in love with could never be his.

Chapter Thirteen

The next morning, Lucas got dressed next to Ruby in silence. Everything left unsaid hung in the air between them, even though the time for talking had passed. The clock was ticking. They had to call off the wedding and he had to get Ruby off Fare Island so that whatever happened after the Silver Knights took Henriksen into custody wouldn't blow back on her. Keeping her close to him wouldn't be loving her, it would be signing her death warrant.

"Ready to go jump off the fjords?" Ruby asked, already heading for the bedroom door.

Lucas swallowed the protest building up inside him and gave her a curt nod. The urge to take her in his arms and kiss her nearly overwhelmed him, but he couldn't give in. His part of the mission was complete. The Silver Knights were setting up in Luxembourg now, prepping the site for Henriksen's arrival in a few days. He was needed back at headquarters, and she needed to be anywhere but here. The longer he kept her here, the more danger she was in, and he refused to leave her like that.

Seeming to understand the personal battle he waged, she gave him a trembling, bittersweet smile before letting out a deep breath and opening the door. They walked down the hall, stopping in unison at the top of the stairs.

There were people everywhere. The foyer was crowded with wedding guests, their chatter and polite laughter filling the air all the way up to the top of the cathedral ceiling.

"I didn't realize everyone would be arriving *en masse* this morning," Ruby said, worry forming sharp lines across her forehead. "So much for making a quiet announcement to my mom and Rolf before the guests arrived."

The fact that more than one hundred people, coming in from all over Northern Europe, had ended up arriving at nearly the exact same time set off Lucas's sixth sense. It couldn't be a coincidence. What it was, he didn't have a clue. He'd figure it out later. Ruby's safety came first.

"This doesn't make it any easier, but we've got to get you off this island." He glanced around at the sea of people. "Do you see your parents?"

"Over there in the corner." She nodded her chin to the right. "Rolf is talking to the short man in the navy suit with his back to us. Mom is listening to that woman wearing the purple fascinator."

Hand in hand, they went down the stairs and wound their way through the well-wishers until they were right behind her parents still deep in conversation with the short man.

"Relax." Rolf clapped his hand hard on the other man's shoulder. "This was the perfect idea. The package arrived with thirty other yachts and smaller crafts. Even if they're watching, they'll never have any idea what's on board. I'm telling you, the wedding is the perfect cover."

Lucas jerked to a stop. All the little details about the short man came into focus. The faded scar above his shirt collar. His super-short blond hair. The chunk missing from the shell of his right ear where a stray bullet during the Elskov coup ten years ago had missed ending the man who would threaten her safety again to avenge his father.

Gregers Henriksen was on Fare Island.

An icy fury directed only at himself pricked every nerve until Lucas was so overloaded, he couldn't feel a damn thing, and this was what let him clearly think for the first time since Ruby had walked past him into Moad Manor. Using the arrival of the wedding guests, a mix of the rich and reckless along with the criminal and shady, to camouflage the arms exchange was the perfect plan. One Lucas should have seen coming. Now there was no way to cancel the wedding, not if he was going to stop that exchange before Henriksen took off with the rest of the guests Sunday morning. Looking over at Ruby, he saw the same stark realization in her eyes.

"It's okay," she whispered. "It comes first."

Before he could form words, Ingrid pivoted and spotted them.

"If it isn't the happy couple," she exclaimed. "Ruby and Luc, come meet Annabelle DiStario, she is Mr. Henriksen's guest and the only woman I've ever met who can do such a beautiful fascinator justice. Don't you agree, Ruby?"

"Most definitely." Her voice shook the slightest bit, but her gaze and welcoming smile held steady as she reached out to shake the woman's hand.

"Have you met Luc Svendsen before, Gregers?" Rolf leaned in closer to the man. "He's a friend of ours who carries secrets for the same reasons the other people carry cash."

Rolf chuckled at his own joke. Ignoring his host, Henriksen narrowed his eyes and gave Lucas the kind of hard look that made every hair on the back of his neck stand at attention. Less than fifteen people in the world knew Luc Svendsen, dealer of information people would rather keep quiet, was Lucas Bendtsen, head of the Silver Knights. The chance of that secret getting out was minute, but who better than him to know that those were the exact kind of secrets that always managed to get out. In the blink of an eye, though, the questioning look disappeared.

"You do look familiar, but I'm having trouble connecting the name with the face." Henriksen shook Lucas's hand. "You'll have to forgive me. I'm horrible with names."

"It's good to meet you." Not wiping his palm on his pants took more self-restraint than he was used to exerting, but control was his best weapon right now.

More of the guests wandered over to extend their well-wishes. The conversation went on around him, and he was sure to make the appropriate responses and facial expressions, but he wasn't really listening. Henriksen had disappeared into the crowd, but Lucas couldn't shake the feeling that the man was somewhere watching him, biding his time. Rolf had already moved the exchange once. Lucas couldn't take the chance that he'd do it again, not when Henriksen and the guns were on the island.

The guns.

It jolted through him. His team wasn't here, but if he, Clausen, and Jasper could confirm their location, the Silver Knights could confiscate them and take Henriksen into custody. The fact that Rolf wouldn't be sentenced to a life inside an Elskovian prison for his part in the plot burned a hole in Lucas's gut, but the order had come down from the queen herself not to touch him. Before any of that, though, he needed to ensure he wasn't sending his agents on another wild goose chase. He had to make sure the guns were here, somewhere on the island.

Ruby intertwined her fingers with his and squeezed. "Don't be fooled by his silence, Ms. DiStario, I'm sure Luc has an interesting take on the latest wool crisis." She looked up at him, tension evident in her strained expression. "Don't you, dear?"

Of course I don't. Who the hell cares about wool when there is an entire armory of guns secreted away somewhere?

And he knew just the person to help him figure out where.

Turning on the charm, he lifted Ruby's hand to his lips and brushed a kiss across her knuckles. "I hate to do this with all the guests arriving, Ingrid, but I have to sneak away with my bride to be for a little bit before you steal her away from me for all the last minute wedding preparations."

"How romantic," DiStario said with a sigh.

Ingrid's face softened, and the underlying sadness that always seemed just under the surface and the spark of iron she'd shown the other night rose to the forefront for half a second before her usual half-hazy expression fell back into place. "You do that. I'll try and hold off the horde for as long as possible."

"Thanks, Mom."

Ruby gave her mother a quick kiss on the cheek before they took off together, hurrying through the kitchen and out the side door onto the deserted staff patio. After a quick look around without spotting anyone, he took another few steps out into the garden and pulled her behind a tall trio of shrubs.

"He changed the exchange," Ruby said, her voice low.

"Looks that way, but I need confirmation before I pull an entire team away from Luxembourg." Really, it was pretty fucking ingenious. Even if the Silver Knights had known the delivery would have happened this way, there was no way they could have stopped and searched each of the vessels arriving at Fare Island without causing a huge international incident. "If it were me, I'd use the arrival of all the wedding guests like camouflage, but I wouldn't want to keep a yacht docked with the others, too many prying criminal eyes, *and* I'd want to be able to have it guarded without drawing attention of the guests or anyone who might be monitoring by satellite."

The satellite imagery of the island showed several narrow inlets, but none looked to be large enough for a yacht to tuck into.

"Skjult Bay. It's small but deep. You could moor a yacht without any problems. There's an abandoned lighthouse there that I used to hide in as a kid. You could use that to minimize the chance of anyone noticing the security sitting around."

"That's it." The maps showed it as the largest cove. It was at the north end of the island, but without being able to go as the crow flies, it would take him twice as long to get there via the winding narrow roads circling the island. "Tell me the Sparrow showed you a shortcut during one of your weird bonding hikes."

She grinned, her gray eyes sparkling with excitement. "There's not a single millimeter of this island I don't know. Come on. We don't have time to waste."

His gut twisted at the idea of putting her in a worse position than she was already in by having to delay getting off the island. "You're not coming with me. It's not safe. Just tell me how to get there."

"You think I'm safer in that place?" She waved a hand toward the main house that was filled with some of the most dangerous people in Northern Europe. "I've never been safer than when I'm with you. You're not going to let anything happen to me, right?"

Even the idea of it made bile rise in his throat. "Never."

She kissed him, just a quick sweep of her lips across his, and he knew he'd never had a chance to win this argument. "Then let's go."

It only took a couple of minutes to get to the garage and swipe the keys to one of the all-terrain vehicles. From there it was a ten-minute drive over land and through an apple orchard to end up on the north coast inland from Skjult Bay. Leaving the ATV in the orchard, they snuck down toward the rocky shore and took up a surveillance spot behind a pair of boulders, peeking around it to spot a single yacht anchored in the bay.

Adrenaline roaring through his veins, he held a finger to his lips and then pointed to her and the spot where her feet were, motioning for her to stay put. He had to get closer, but he wasn't going to risk her to do so. After she gave him a grimace and a nod, he hustled down to a rocky outcropping closer to the water's edge.

Ruby's guess had been spot-on. From his new location, he could see guards stationed outside the door of the tall, stone lighthouse, a trio standing under the yacht's deck awning, and a few scattered stacks of automatic-weapon-sized crates on board.

Between the guns secured in the smuggler's hold of his jet and Jasper, Clausen, and himself, they could maintain surveillance until the Silver Knights could arrive with the firepower to end the exchange before it had a chance to begin.

He grabbed his phone so he could alert Clausen and he turned to make his way back to Ruby. Something set off his inner alarms. He glanced up from the screen and stopped cold. It took a second for the scene to make sense in his head, and then the pieces tumbled together as the air drained out of his lungs.

Four yards away, Henriksen stood next to Rolf. Both were behind Ruby. Rolf had his Beretta 9mm pointed at the back of her head. The entire world narrowed down to a pinpoint with Ruby at the center and time slowed to a stop.

Your orders are simple. Discover the exchange location. Stop it. Save Elskov. The words were a scream in his head.

Henricksen was unarmed and had the panicked aura of a rabbit gone motionless. Lucas could take him. He could kill the bastard with his bare hands before he ever made it to the gun-packed yacht, but he couldn't do it before Rolf pulled his trigger.

Ruby stood directly across from him, watching him with that damned bittersweet smile he fucking detested, the one that said it's okay, screw me over, I knew it would happen eventually and have accepted it.

He tensed his muscles to walk forward into battle. The words came louder this time, so much his ears rang.

Your orders are simple.

Discover the exchange location.

Stop it.

Save Elskov.

There was nothing there about civilian casualties, nothing about saving Ruby—nothing about how to live with himself after. If Rolf didn't kill her now, he would before Lucas could get back to Fare Island to save her. There was fear in her eyes but a determined tightness in her jaw. She was fighting the panic, but his girl was scared and she should be. She knew the stakes from the first moment he blackmailed her to put her life on the line so he could accomplish his mission.

Fuck his orders. He'd find another way to take down Henricksen. And as for Rolf? He was a dead man, he just didn't know it yet. Lucas took a step forward, putting every bit of menace in that single movement he'd ever learned over a lifetime of fighting the odds all so he could betray the country that had saved him in order to save the woman he loved.

Rolf let out an acidic chuckle. "Women. They always push us into the wrong decision, don't they, Luc?" He shoved the gun's muzzle hard against Ruby's temple. "Gregers, I have this. Go ahead and take the yacht."

"Shoot him," Henriksen demanded. "I'm not leaving witnesses, especially not a Silver Knight."

"No one dies on my island without my say so." An angry flush turned Rolf's cheeks red. "Don't press it, Gregers. I promise you won't like the result."

The other man hesitated, hate hardening his features, but after a few moments of indecision, stalked off toward the yacht. A small voice inside Lucas's head yelled that he needed to follow Henriksen and take down his number one target, but there was no way he was going anywhere without Ruby.

Keeping his gaze hard and his stance loose, he considered the possibilities. Without a weapon there weren't many options to be had. He couldn't rush Rolf, not with his gun pressed against Ruby's head, but he could distract the crime boss and draw his fire.

He took another threatening step forward. "Let her go."

"Or what, you'll glare me to death?" Rolf snarled. "I'm the only one with a gun here."

The fool thought he couldn't take a man apart with only his hands? "No, what I'll do will be slow, painful, and leave you wishing I'd just blown your fucking head off."

"The only one losing their head today will be you and this bit of fluff who was stupid enough to bring a Silver Knight on my island." Rolf glanced down at Ruby who, even as scared as she was, looked ready to spit in his eye. "I've been waiting for this moment since I first laid eyes on you, girl."

"Lucas, go!" Ruby screamed as she twisted and grabbed Rolf's arm, shoving it upward.

That wasn't going to happen. He charged toward Rolf. The other man's eyes widened, and he fought off Ruby, shoving her to the ground. He brought the gun up and aimed the Beretta at Lucas.

A shot boomed.

Blood spurted from one side of Rolf's temple and chunks of pink from the other. The crime boss dropped to his knees, way past dead before what was left of his head hit the grass. Lucas swerved around Ruby and grabbed Rolf's gun from his dead grip, whirled around, and pointed toward the orchard where the kill shot had originated.

Ingrid stood there, her face grim. The Sparrow took the gun from her limp grasp.

Despite the training to go after his main target, Lucas gathered the woman he loved in his arms. Even as he watched Gregers and the yacht loaded down with a cache of arms make its way out into the Northern Atlantic, he knew there was no other place he could be right now.

"We've got to get moving, if you're going to stop that boat before it gets to Elskov," the Sparrow said. "I suggest we take care of it at my cabin."

Chapter Fourteen

Ruby clung to Lucas on the ATV ride through the orchard and along the back roads to the Sparrow's cabin. The speed and the wind prevented them from talking, but the tension in his body screamed louder than words. He should have gone after Gregers, but he'd stayed with her.

How would the queen interpret that? Disloyalty? Treason? What price would he pay for not following orders? There was always a price; she'd grown up seeing people pay dearly for slights much smaller than this one. She refused to let Lucas pay the price for her—she loved him too much for that. The best thing she could do for him was to get out of his life before she hurt him anymore.

As soon as they reached the Sparrow's cabin, she hopped off the back of the ATV and hustled into the house ahead of him. The sound of gunfire could be heard in the distance. It wouldn't be long before her stepfather's minions stormed through the cabin door, determined to protect the remaining Macintoshes. She didn't know how she was going to do it, but she had to convince him to go after Gregers now. If he didn't, he'd regret it for the rest of his life.

Jasper and Talia were already inside, both looking fierce and ready for a fight.

"He's dead?" Jasper asked, looking from Ruby to her mother.

Ingrid nodded. "I need to talk to both of you. Alone. Now."

"Take the bedroom," the Sparrow said. "I'll get these two set up. Sounds like most of the island knows already. Every one of the paranoid bastards at the house is going to think it was a plot by the person sitting next to them, and they'll all come out guns blazing, thinking they're next on the hit list. At that point, we'll be lucky to find a port in the shitstorm."

Before she could say anything to Lucas, her mother herded her and Jasper into the bedroom and shut the door behind them. Like the rest of the cabin, it was small and Spartan. There was barely enough room for the three of them to stand in a small circle in the tiny space between the door and the bed.

Her mother had just killed a man and instead of looking like she was about to fall apart like Ruby expected, Ingrid was 100 percent in lioness-protecting-her-cubs mode.

"We don't have a lot of time, but I can't leave without you both knowing the truth. I should have told you before but... well, I failed you there and I'm sorry." Ingrid took a deep breath, a steely determination in her eyes. "When I met Rolf I was a young mother married to a very bad man who finally delivered one beating too many. I killed him before he could do the same to me."

Ruby reached out for Jasper. His hand clamped around hers as she tried to make sense of her mother's words.

Ingrid took in a shaky breath. "Rolf had been around for months at this point. He was always there when I turned around, like a guardian angel, stepping in when your father started getting angry and drunk, distracting him from his favorite target, me. Afterward, Rolf got me out of there. I was dumb enough to think he was doing it because he loved me. He didn't love me. He was obsessed with having me. There is a definite difference, one I didn't learn until years later when it was far too late. By the time I figure it out, I realized that I was trapped here and so were you. He held the possible murder charge over my head to keep me on Fare Island, and once the threat of that lost its power, he promised that if I ever left he'd kill you both."

Her mother's confession rattled around in her head like a pinball, crashing into forgotten memories and knocking them over so she could see them from a different perspective. Her mother's depression. Her insistence on them always doing as Rolf asked. His preoccupation with controlling all of them. He'd threatened her mother with her life as much as he'd threatened Ruby with ruining Ingrid's happiness. No doubt he'd dangled both of them in front of Jasper.

She turned to her brother. He was as slack jawed as she was.

Ingrid reached out and grabbed their hands. "I know you've each been trying to get out in your own way, and I've done what I can to help. The initial contact with the Americans while you were at college, Jasper? The Sparrow helped me arrange it. And Rolf finally giving in and allowing you to live off the island, Ruby? That took a lot of maneuvering, but we made it happen. Now that he's dead, none of us have to worry about him ever again."

"I don't understand, why did you stay once we were older?" Ruby asked, trying desperately to understand a woman she'd thought she'd always known. "You've had opportunities—the trips to Paris or to Elskov."

"I couldn't, not until I knew you both were safe. Especially not with the mad game the both of you were playing with this whole fake wedding business," she said.

"You knew?" she and Jasper both asked at the same time.

Ingrid laughed. "I'm your mother. I always know what you two are up to."

"So what happens now?" Jasper asked.

"We get off this island, and after that, it's up to you. You're free. We're all free." Ingrid pulled her children in for a quick hug. "What do you want?"

What Ruby wanted, she couldn't have — not all of it. Rolf being dead didn't change the fact that the Silver Knights would never be able to see her as anything other than a criminal's daughter and the reason why Gregers made it off Fare Island, and they wouldn't be wrong. Lucas may think it wouldn't matter, but the Silver Knights were his family, and eventually he'd resent her and hate himself for it. She refused to let that happen.

"I want to start over," she said. A new place. A new life. It's all she'd ever dreamed of and it was the last thing she wanted.

"I can make that happen," Jasper said. "But it's going to hurt."

. . .

Lucas shrugged on the bulletproof vest Talia handed up from the storage unit hidden behind a false wall in the cabin. The Sparrow hadn't been wrong. The sound of shots could be heard in the distance. The shooters would make their way here eventually. The cabin was on the way to the dock and the airstrip. If his shitty luck held, one of the Macintosh crew would be by to deliver the bad news about Rolf to the Sparrow and tell him to start sharpening his knives.

Still, even knowing that, he kept his attention focused on the bedroom door, waiting for it to open and Ruby to come out.

"You gonna keep staring a hole in that door, or are you going to pick a damn gun?" The Sparrow pointed at the gun rack filled to capacity.

"I'll take the Uzi." If he was going to have to fight his way to his jet on the airstrip in the midst of total anarchy, he wanted something that fired six hundred bullets a minute.

The Sparrow handed him the submachine gun as the bedroom door opened. Ruby walked out with her mom and brother. The moment she spotted him, she went still and two pink spots bloomed on her cheeks. His sixth sense went into overdrive. Whatever was coming next, he wasn't going to like it.

"Are you ready, Hamish?" Ingrid asked.

The Sparrow nodded. "Yep. You've said your good-byes?"

She wiped away a tear and nodded.

"Okay then." He opened the pantry and pulled a hidden latch to reveal a set of stairs. "Down through the tunnel. Follow me, and we'll end up at Frihed Inlet. I've got a boat waiting."

Ingrid gave Jasper and Ruby each a long hug, whispering something he couldn't hear and then followed the Sparrow down the secret staircase, pulling the trap door shut with a final thunk.

Classen pressed her finger to the comm unit in her ear. "Copy that." She turned to him. "Sir, the exfil unit is five minutes out. We have to go now."

As soon as the first gunshots sounded outside the cabin, he'd known getting to the tarmac with Ruby was going to be too dangerous so he'd mobilized the offsite team commanding them to a rendezvous point away from the tarmac and dock. "Let's go."

Jasper shook his head. "And miss a once in a lifetime opportunity like this? The agency is going to love having a double agent of their own with access to everything the Macintosh organization knows."

Fuck. He didn't like it, but he understood it. The Americans would have access to information about all of the arms and drug deals happening in Northern Europe that were being used to fund terrorist activities. Turning down that opportunity would be insane.

"Understood," he said, then turned to Clausen. "Looks like you're riding solo."

Clausen's gaze lingered on Jasper for a heartbeat longer than necessary before she hustled out the backdoor without a word and climbed on one of the ATVs, ready to make a run for the airstrip.

He crossed the room and reached out for Ruby's hands, but she kept them clasped in front of her.

She shook her head. "I'm staying."

Two words that hit harder than a heavyweight punch. "Ruby—"

Another round of gunfire interrupted him. This time it was closer and accompanied by shouts.

"I'll watch out for her. You don't have time to argue." Jasper said. "I can slow down the first wave of Macintosh soldiers, but they'll be looking to sequester anyone who's not family by any means necessary. You'll have a five-minute head start, and after that, it's all up to you."

Oh, he'd make it out of here, and he'd do it with Ruby on that jet.

"I'm not going anywhere without you."

She gave him that sad smile he really hated. "You have to go. Stop Gregers. Save Elskov. Be the good guy that I know you are."

Those were his orders, the ones he wanted to forget he'd ever accepted. He'd ignored them once already when he didn't have a choice. But Jasper was right, with Rolf out of the picture, the other man could keep Ruby safe, for now. She wouldn't be totally safe until Henriksen was out of the picture. For Elskov and for Ruby, he'd track the traitorous asshole down and sink him for good.

Your orders are simple.

Track down Henriksen's yacht.

Seize it.

Save Elskov.

Spend the rest of your life with Ruby.

Be the hero. Get the girl. Isn't that how it worked for the good guys Ruby swore he was one of?

He pulled Ruby close, memorizing every little detail about her in that single heartbeat, and brushed his lips across hers. "I'm coming back for you."

"You have to go first," she murmured, tears glistening in her eyes.

He took her mouth in a kiss meant to say everything he couldn't and promise everything he'd deliver in the future, and there would be one. He'd do whatever it took to make sure of that. Hating that he had to do so, he broke the kiss and pocketed an extra magazine for the Uzi.

"This isn't over," Lucas said, then ran out the door, guns ready.

• • •

It took everything Ruby had not to follow Lucas out the door. Watching him leave wrecked her, but she didn't have a choice, not if the plan she'd concocted with Jasper was going to work. She watched from the window as the ATVs' dust trails disappeared, praying she'd made the right decision not just for him, but for her, too.

"Are you sure about this?" Jasper asked, taking a handgun from the rack before handing her a bulletproof vest.

She took the vest, which was much heavier than it appeared, and slipped it on. "Are you?"

"I made my choice when I agreed to work with the Americans." He fastened the Velcro on the vest and handed her a sweatshirt he'd brought with him from the Sparrow's room. "You've never had a choice. You were too busy watching out for everyone else to watch out for yourself. That shit better end now."

Damn, he was going to make her cry. "You're not as dumb as you look, little brother."

"I had a really great older sister who taught me some things."

She watched him as he crossed to the kitchen, more than a little bit awed at the brain and guile he'd been hiding all these years. With his chin-length blond hair, olive complexion, and relaxed, come-what-may vibe, he'd always seemed more American surfer than Nordic. He'd used his looks for a cover so well, and for so long, that he'd even fooled her into believing he was just a pretty face, but not anymore. From now on things were going to be different between them.

While he filled a plastic baggie with a mix of ketchup and water, she tugged the sweatshirt on over her head. He disappeared from view when she tugged the sweatshirt on over her head and his voice was muffled. "Are you sure you want to do this? Is he worth it?"

She pulled the sweatshirt into place and Jasper's face came back into view. "Starting over without any of Rolf's bullshit tied around my neck, that's all for me, but if it wasn't?" An image of Lucas last night popped into her head. "Yeah, he'd be worth it. I have to do this for him. It's for his own good. You'll make him understand."

The sound of shouting outside filtered in.

"For you? Anything." He tossed her the baggie, strode to the window, and peeked out front. "I can see the tops of their heads over the gate."

"So let's do this." She slipped the baggie under her sweatshirt and secured it to the bulletproof vest.

The *pop*, *pop*, *pop* of gunfire could be heard just outside the door.

Jasper lifted the gun, his mouth set in a grim line. "This is going to hurt like hell."

Oh goodie. Exactly what every girl wanted to hear. She took a deep breath. "Do it."

He pulled the trigger. A freight train slammed into her chest. Warm liquid seeped out over her shirt. She went down. Her head bounced against the floor hard enough to rattle her teeth. Thirty seconds later, the door crashed open and the floor vibrated from the thunder of Macintosh guards running to Jasper.

"He shot her and ran out the back!" Jasper shouted. "Go get the bastard."

"Is she okay?" one of the men asked.

"Does she look okay?" The question came out as a viscous snarl. "The motherfucker just killed my sister. Bring him back alive. I'm going to fillet the bastard. Go!"

Footsteps pounded. The backdoor slammed shut. Then there was silence.

"They're gone."

She opened her eyes and raised her arm so he could help her up, wincing in pain. "Laying it on a little thick weren't you?"

"I've been doing this double-agent thing quite a bit longer than you. I know what it takes." He scooped her up in his arms as if he did that type of thing all the time and headed toward the front door. "Time to play dead again. We gotta make sure as many people as possible see me run to the main house with dead you in my arms so when you start over in Montana or Maine no one has any idea. It has to look real. With any luck, the bad-guy grapevine will have your obit posted before the day's out."

"Are you going to cry?"

Jasper grinned down at her. "I'm going to fucking weep, gnash my teeth, and promise to burn the whole world down to avenge you. They thought Rolf was bad. Just wait until they get a load of me."

The poor fools had no idea.

· · ·

Thirty-thousand feet above the North Atlantic Ocean on the Silver Knights mobile command jet, Lucas noted, but didn't give a shit, that everyone had breathed a sigh of relief when he'd locked himself into his small office in the back of the plane. Tension had chewed a hole in his gut and worry was chipping away at what was left.

He hated not being in the group of agents boarding Henriksen's ship right now. He loathed being in any plane he wasn't piloting. He despised that all he could do was pace and watch the clock until word came in that the operation had been a success. More than all of that though, he couldn't stand being away from Ruby.

He didn't give a shit what anyone said, as soon as this mission wrapped up, he was going to find her. If that meant the end of his term as head of the Silver Knights, so be it. He may owe his life to Elskov, but his heart belonged to Ruby.

Three quick raps sounded on his office door.

"Enter."

Clausen walked in, armed with a clipboard and a grim expression.

"We have him, sir," Clausen said. "The Elskov Royal Navy picked him up. His boat may have been loaded down with guns and ammunition, but it was no match for a battleship."

Good news, which didn't explain the way she couldn't meet his gaze. He grasped for possibilities. Could Rolf have double-crossed Henriksen? Were the guns in the wind? That was the last thing they needed.

He grabbed the bottle of antacids on his desk and shook out a few tablets into his hand. "And the weapons?"

She consulted the clipboard as if she didn't know the answer already. "Confiscated and on their way to a secure location."

"So what's wrong?" He popped the tablets into his mouth, knowing even as he did so that they weren't going to alleviate the worry churning in his stomach. "Don't tell me the Americans are elbowing in this operation any more than they already have."

"No." She shook her head. "There's been a fire at the main house on Fare Island."

His lungs twisted into a tight knot and he lost the ability to take a breath. "Was anyone hurt?"

"Our reports are that everyone made it out."

Only years of training kept him from collapsing into his chair with relief. "Thank God."

Finally, Clausen made eye contact, and he suddenly wished like hell that she'd kept her attention on that damn clipboard. She had the same look in her eyes he'd seen as a kid when the upstairs neighbor had meet him outside his apartment to let him know his mother had overdosed.

"One of the low-level thugs in the Macintosh organization told one of our informants that Ruby Macintosh had been shot and killed prior to the fire. Her body was in the house at the time of the blaze. They weren't able to retrieve her remains before the house became fully engulfed."

There may have been more words. He didn't hear them. He just stood there, frozen as his world fell apart. Gone. He should have stayed. He should have protected her. He should have listened to his heart. Now it was too late.

Clausen cleared her throat. "I'm sorry, sir."

Fuck. How long had she been standing there? A minute? Ten? Longer? He had no clue. "Thank you for letting me know."

"Of course, sir." She nodded and left.

He crossed to the built-in filing cabinet and yanked open the top drawer. Inside was a bottle of akvavit and a set of small glasses. It was for special celebrations at the end of a successful mission. He'd done his duty. Put Elskov first.

Today was a success.

Henriksen was out of the picture.

He took out the bottle and a single glass. The arms deal had been thwarted. He poured a double shot, not bothering with ice.

The guns were confiscated.

He picked up the glass and held it to his lips, unable to take a single sip.

Ruby was dead because of him, because he'd blackmailed her to save Elskov and it had worked. Beautifully.

All the color faded from his surroundings. The last to go was the gray of Ruby's eyes, leaving only pristine and orderly lines of black and white that never crossed and never mixed and never made him whole.

Today was a success.

He flung the glass across the room. It shattered against the wall, sending shards of glass flying everywhere. Lifting the bottle to his lips, he took a swig and relished the burn as he watched the splattered liquid drip down the wall as useless for getting drunk as he was for keeping Ruby safe.

Chapter Fifteen

Three days later, Lucas poured himself a glass of akvavit and waited for the Elskov State Seal on the video screen in his office to fade away and reveal the queen. It was his last official duty as head of the Silver Knights. After she accepted his resignation, he'd be free to pass the security codes on to Clausen and walk away from Moad Manor, from the Silver Knights, from Elskov.

The screen went black for half a second before the king appeared with the queen by his side.

"Your Majesties," Lucas said, bowing his head in deference for the absolute minimum amount of time before looking up and taking another drink.

The alcohol's burn did nothing to minimize the pain of seeing them together—the queen with her pregnancy glow and the king standing beside her, always at her side and so obviously in love that Lucas barely recognized the hard, uncompromising Dominick Rasmussen he'd worked with for eight years. He'd never resented their happiness before, but now it was gravel in an open wound.

"Your resignation is not accepted," the queen said, annoyance and worry evident in her tone.

As if anything could stop him. "I'm going anyway."

"Is it because of the asset?" the king asked, ignoring th shocked gasp of his queen. "What was her name? Renee? Rosie? Rita?"

"You know damn well it's Ruby Macintosh." It was the first time since Fare Island that he'd said her name out loud and it cost him, chipping away at the akvavit ice he'd encased himself in.

"That's the one," the king said, continuing despite the wide-eyed, shut-up-you-idiot look from the queen. "Nasty business her ending up dead. Casualties can happen in any operation, that's not a reason to quit. She was, after all, just an asset."

Because he'd drunk enough to be flammable, the explosion shouldn't have shocked Lucas, but it did. The heat seared him from the inside out. The anger sent his heart rate into overdrive. The self-hatred and blame battered against his bones.

"She was not just an asset!" The words tore from him half howl, half roar.

"Exactly, and it's about time you admitted it," the king replied, his blasé attitude replaced with genuine sympathy, no doubt he thought jabbing a finger into Lucas's open wound was necessary to prove a point. "And that's why you submitted your resignation. It has nothing to do with how you did your job and everything to do with the loss you suffered for us."

"My reasons for resigning are clearly stated in my letter." With more care than he'd used to protect the woman he'd loved, Lucas set his tumbler of akvavit down on the desk that wouldn't be his for much longer. "I disregarded my orders. I chose Ruby over Elskov, Henriksen nearly got away with the guns."

The empathy in the queen's eyes nearly undid him. "But he didn't."

No he hadn't. Something just as bad had happened.

"After that, I followed my orders and left her behind so she could be killed." He hadn't pulled the trigger, but he may as well have. He didn't know where he was going. He didn't know what he would do. He didn't know how he'd ever be able to go on without her. But he knew one thing as sure as he knew he'd fucked up beyond redemption. "I can't blindly follow orders anymore."

"Whoever said we wanted you to?" the king asked, frustration booming in each word.

Lucas snapped to attention. "It's the soldier's way."

"You're not a soldier anymore. Elskov can't afford to see things in terms of black and white anymore if it's going to succeed," the queen said. "And if the Silver Knights aren't just a fancy version of gray in a black and white world, then I don't know who would be."

The words sounded so much like something Ruby would have said, he reached for the glass to numb himself. "She's gone."

"She is and I am so sorry for that, but do you really think she'd want you to give up your family and lose yourself in a bottle?" The queen pointed at the half-empty decanter on the desk.

"My family?" Lucas didn't have any family. Really, he never had.

"Us. Elskov," she said. "You can't just walk away when we need you."

He sat the glass back on his desk untouched. "I'll think about it."

The queen nodded. "I know you'll make the right choice. You always do."

"And Bendtsen," the king said. "We really are sorry about Ruby. I can't even imagine what you're going through, but we're here for you, even when it may not seem like it."

In that heartbeat he knew he couldn't leave. He was as

much a part of Elskov as it was a part of him. This is what Ruby had meant that night at dinner when he'd asked her why she hadn't just walked away from her family and started fresh. He finally understood—you couldn't leave family behind, not even if you physically walked away.

"Thank you, Your Majesty."

"It's Dom, Lucas." He gave him a gruff smile. "And there's no need for thanks. That's what family does."

· · ·

Later that evening, Lucas sat in the sitting room in Moad Manor and poured another glass of akvavit and another and another. He should be drunk by now. That's what he wanted, to finally fall into oblivion so that he couldn't even remember Ruby's name or hear the soft moan she made or smell the exotic scent of her perfume. But it didn't work. He was stone sober staring out at the garden and the chairs sitting out in the field of lavender barely visible because of the clouds blocking most of the light from the new moon.

Staring out, his eyes tired and unfocused, he nearly missed it but years of training worked when the rest of him didn't. The glint of moonlight off something metallic. The sudden silence. The extrasensory awareness creeping up the back of his neck.

A holdout from Hendriksen's camp?

A rogue Macintosh operator?

He was a man with enemies. It didn't matter who had finally tracked him down because without Ruby he had nothing to lose and he was itching for a fight, for someone to bear the brunt of the fury burning a hole in his gut. There was nothing more dangerous.

Keeping his movements controlled but natural, he crossed to the open French doors and strolled out into the garden, keeping his face tilted up toward the night sky even as he scoped out the area with his peripheral vision.

His gut tightened a half a second before the snap of a twig off to his left.

He pivoted and launched himself at the intruder. His shoulder connected with something hard. They went down in a tangle of limbs, but he managed to land on top of his opponent, whose face was hidden by the night's shadows. It didn't matter. He pulled back his arm, ready to deliver a knockout blow.

"Lucas, it's me."

And just like that, Ruby KO'd him without lifting a finger.

• • •

Ruby cringed as Lucas scrambled up off her as if she was radioactive and she couldn't blame him. She was as bad for him as anything that set off a Geiger counter. Giving in to the urge to see Lucas one last time had been a mistake. If she'd just disappeared into an American big city, Ruby could have saved him this, but she'd been weak. She'd thought sneaking a peek of him one last time would ease the marrow-deep misery of leaving him forever. He wasn't supposed to see her. She should have left the garden half an hour ago, but as soon as she'd spotted him pouring himself a drink alone she hadn't been able to take even a single step away.

"I'm sorry. I'm so very sorry." She got up and shoved her hands in the pockets of her black jeans to keep from reaching out for him. "I should have left before now."

Walk away, Ruby. Leave. Get out of here before you can't.

He didn't make a move toward her. Was that the best thing to have happened or the worst? No fucking clue. Everything hurt too much to know. They just stared at each other. She took in all the details. The dark circles under his bloodshot eyes. His unshaven jaw. The overall haggard weariness in his stance. Whatever revenge the queen had inflicted for Lucas disobeying her orders, it obviously had affected him deeply.

"You're alive," he said, taking half a step closer before stopping himself. "It doesn't make sense. I heard the report from Clausen. I saw the satellite imagery showing the fire and the burning husk of the house after it was over."

They hadn't planned that part, but it covered their tracks better than anything they could have done. "Jasper and I faked my death."

That statement of the obvious broke through whatever shock had wrapped itself around Lucas. His entire body went ridged and he stalked toward her, a predator stalking its prey with every intention of shredding its prey.

Lucas stopped an arm's reach away from her, everything about him wound tight. "Why would you do that?"

The question was quiet, so quiet it sent a frightened shiver up her spine. "I did it for you."

"For me?" He punctuated his words with a booming laugh that made a mockery of the joy normally associated with the sound.

This wasn't Lucas, not her Lucas anyway. This was her fault. The attitude, the underlying anger. If she hadn't fallen so hard for him, she would have been able to keep her distance, but even now staying away from him seemed almost impossible. She had to make him understand.

"I couldn't let you make any more sacrifices for me." She reached out for him, but he brushed off her touch. "I knew you'd pay a price for disobeying your orders if I stayed around. No matter what, I'll always be the crime boss's daughter and you're the head of the Silver Knights. I'd ruin everything for you. I wanted to protect you from that."

"So letting me think that I'd killed you was your way of protecting me? I know growing up at Rolf Macintosh's knee would fuck a person up, but this is so far beyond that."

She flinched. His words hit as hard as a slap. "I couldn't let you know. If you had, you would have tried to stop me."

The breeze ruffled her now black hair, tugging it from the ponytail she'd pulled it into and she held her breath. The last thing she could take was the scent of lavender—something she'd always associate with Lucas for the rest of her life—as he looked at her as if she was the worst human being on earth. She'd known it would happen. He'd realize just how bad she was for him, but she hadn't thought she'd be there to see it. The reality of it was so much worse than what even her twisted imagination could bring to life.

"You know, the first time you walked in here, I steeled myself against you knowing that if I didn't I'd end up like all the other poor saps you'd manipulated, but you managed to play me anyway. I guess I'm lucky that you're the one who ended up dead instead of me."

And this was how it ended. She'd come here hoping to get one last look at the man she loved, share one final moment, even if she was the only one who'd realized what was happening. Instead, she'd proven everything about why she and Lucas could never be together.

She took a step backward, unable to look away from him. "I shouldn't have come."

"No you shouldn't have." Cruel. Harsh. Deserved. "You can't be dead if you're in my garden."

Her feet faltered at the pain in his voice, but the knowledge of why she was doing this steadied her when all she wanted to do was throw herself at him. "I think it's best if we act as if I am."

"Agreed." He nodded, his face as hard as granite. "Because you are dead to me."

Letting the Sparrow have another go at carving up her palm would have hurt less. Hell, having her fingernails pulled out with saltwater-soaked pliers would have done less damage. But this is what it was, what it had to be.

Without another word, she turned and walked away, leaving Lucas staring in his lavender garden, free to be the Silver Knight he was destined to be. She gritted her teeth and forced her feet forward. She'd follow the same path linking the garden to the shore she'd taken to get here. Another pair of painful steps. A boat was waiting for her there. She pushed passed the agony twisting her insides. The captain would take her to Scotland and from there, she'd board another ship to America. She reached for the gate latch. And then—

Lucas's palm slammed against the gate, holding it shut. "You're not going anywhere, not without me."

. . .

Heart thundering in his chest at his own idiocy at how he'd almost lost her again, Lucas took Ruby by the shoulders and spun her around. She looked up at him, her gray eyes gleaming with unshed tears and it gutted him. God, he was a moron. "Neither of us is walking away again. That's not what you do when it's someone you love."

She shook her head. "Lucas, it won't work."

"Not if we don't fight for it." This wasn't his area. He wasn't a charmer. He gave out orders. He marshaled forces. He made plans. He didn't know what to do when it came to convincing the woman he loved to stay. So he did the only thing he could think of. He told her the truth. "Look, I was an ass. Everything I said was awful and wrong. I could blame the shock or the fact that I haven't slept since I'd thought you'd died but the truth of it is I said it because I was scared."

"Of what?"

"That I couldn't take it if I lost you again. I love you. You're smart. You're sexy. You make me want to be the good man you seem to inexplicably think that I am."

Tears spilled down her cheek. "But the queen, she's mad enough at you already."

"Only because I tried to quit."

"I'm still just the crime boss's daughter and if I stay— maybe not now but eventually—you will resent me for ruining your life."

"Without you it's already ruined. This last week has shown me that. It's been worse than hell." For a man who lied for a living, he'd never told so much of the truth in only a few sentences. No matter what. No matter where. They were in this together from here on out. "Damn it, Ruby, I love you. If you're going, so am I."

She choked back a sob as she waved her hand at the house and grounds. "You can't leave this."

Looking around, he took it all in. The gentleman spy. The aristocrat. It wasn't him. For all that his name had changed, he hadn't. At heart, he was still Luc Svendsen, a scrappy kid who survived by his wits and pulled himself up from nothing. She'd seen that way before he ever had.

"Of course I can walk away. It's just a house. It's just a job."

"One that you love." She wiped away her tears with the back of her had. "One that means everything to you."

"Not as much as you do." He pulled her close. She felt good. This felt good. The two of them together were as close to good as he was ever going to get. She had to feel it too. "Don't start over in America. Start over here with me, as my wife, as my partner on the Silver Knights."

Ruby gasped and pushed him away. "That's insane."

"No, it's perfect." And it was, so much that he couldn't believe he hadn't thought of it earlier. It was the perfect solution to everything. "You're smart. You're a survivor. You're determined. You're stubborn as hell. You're perfect for me and for the Silver Knights."

"Just like that? And no one would object to the crime boss's daughter becoming one of the good guys?" she scoffed, but she couldn't hide the excitement in her voice.

"They took me, didn't they?" He tugged her close again, brushing his lips across hers. "Say yes. Say you'll marry me."

. . .

A month later, Ruby was once again in a house populated by armed liars and skilled manipulators of the first order who'd do just about anything to accomplish their mission—but unlike her experiences on Fare Island, they were all doing it for the right reasons.

Just like the first time she'd been in Lucas's office, the Queen of Elskov was on the giant screen taking up a huge chunk of the wall next to a long table. It was a sight Ruby wasn't sure she'd ever get used to. Saying she had nervous butterflies doing the conga in her stomach was putting it lightly.

Unlike before, each seat was taken by a Silver Knight, including Talia Clausen whose long red hair was pinned into a tight bun at the base of her neck.

"Well then," the queen said from the video screen. "If there's nothing else to cover concerning Gregers Henriksen's arrest and upcoming trial, let's move on to the last item on the agenda. I understand we have a new Silver Knight with a rather unusual resume."

Every set of eyes at the table turned to her, including a pair of aquamarine ones that belonged to the man who'd been crazy enough to think this whole thing could work.

"Yes, Your Majesty," Lucas said, squeezing her hand under the table. "You've met Agent Bendtsen."

The queen arched an eyebrow. "I wasn't aware you'd decided to change your name, agent."

"It won't be official until the wedding in a few months," Ruby said, unable to stop the giddy grin that appeared on her face whenever she thought about the fake wedding that was turning out to be real. "But I decided to go ahead and try it on for size now."

"Looks to me like it fits you perfectly," the queen said before giving her a wink. "Now then, if there's nothing else, I'd say we're done here. The people of Elskov may never know all that you've done to keep them safe, but I, for one, am eternally grateful. Thank you."

Everyone at the table stood and bowed toward the screen.

"Ugh, I will never get used to that," the queen grumbled, an embarrassed pink tinting her cheeks. "Go off and do something fun. Royal orders."

The screen flickered and the livestream of the queen was replaced by a static image of the Elskov State Seal.

The other agents around the table gathered their folders and electronic tablets before heading to the door. Talia let out a quiet yawn as she followed the pack, the action emphasizing the dark circles under the woman's normally alert eyes.

She paused in front of Ruby and Lucas. "Three weeks?"

Lucas nodded decisively. "Not a day less."

Talia shot him a glare, but didn't argue. Instead, she followed the rest of the agents out the door.

None of the Silver Knights were what she'd describe as soft touches, but Talia seemed cynical and hardened even for the secret protectors of Elskov. The woman was an uber type A with extra rigid on the side and a generous helping of "don't fuck with me" sprinkled over the top. Ruby couldn't help but feel sorry for the resort staff who'd have to deal with a grumpy Talia on a forced vacation.

"So you're really making her go?" she asked once all the agents were gone and the office door was closed once more. "Can you *do* that?"

"I'm the head of the Silver Knights, I can do anything," Lucas said, as cocky and sure of himself as ever. "Anyway, she hasn't been herself since the last mission."

She suddenly became very interested in sorting the reports in her folder so he wouldn't see the smile she couldn't hide. For all the gruff, no-sense-of-humor, alpha-ness of him, Lucas sure did have a gooey, soft center for the people he cared about.

She cleared her throat to get the giggle out of it. "My brother can drive a person to drink. Being stuck with him twenty-four seven for as long as they were, I'm not surprised she's out of sorts."

"I told her it was either vacation or she'd have to act as the human guinea pig when Osborn needs to test out one of his inventions. I'm sending her to the Bahamas. I hear a certain newly minted crime boss is taking some R&R there."

Ruby whipped her head up and dropped the reports to the table.

There wasn't a trace of shame on his face at returning once again to his old tactics. In fact, he looked pretty damn proud of himself, and she couldn't blame him one little bit.

"Lucas Bendtsen, are you turning into a blackmailing matchmaker?"

He shrugged. "Just watching out for my people and making sure they get what they need."

If she could have fallen any more in love with him, she would have right then and there. "All of your people, huh?" She raised herself up on her tiptoes, bringing her mouth close to his. "Even me?"

"Oh, I know exactly what you need." Desire flared in his gaze and a wicked grin that promised all sorts of happily ever afters curled his lips. "I promise to always make sure you get it."

And he did.

Acknowledgments

This book would have never have come to be if it hadn't been for a crazy phone call with my editor, Alethea Spiridon, who has spent time with me in real life and still talks to me anyway. With that one phone call, the Tempt Me series was born. I couldn't have done it without you. Thanks Alethea!

Another huge thank-you goes out to the entire team at Entangled who helped make this book a reality. Y'all rock my world. A special shout out to my street team, The Flynnbots, who post very motivational photos of extremely hot men. They really are doing the Lord's work.

As always, many thanks going out to the fantastically talented Kimberly Kincaid and Robin Covington who are responsible for all of my bad habits. Every. Single. One. For real. :)

And, of course, I couldn't have done any of this without my family's support. So to the Fab Mr. Flynn who pretends to believe me when I say "THIS time I'm not going to be twenty thousand words short two weeks before deadline" and to the three Flynn kids who never met a closed office door they wouldn't burst through anyway: I love you guys.

xoxo, Avery

About the Author

Avery Flynn is an award winning romance author. She has three slightly-wild children, loves a hockey-addicted husband and is desperately hoping someone invents the coffee IV drip. She was a reader before she was a writer and hopes to always be both. She loves to write about smartass alpha heroes who are as good with a quip as they are with their *ahem* other God-given talents. Her heroines are feisty, fierce, and fantastic. Brainy and brave, these ladies know how to stand on their own two feet and knock the bad guys off theirs. Subscribe to her newsletter for all her latest book news. Find out more about Avery on her website, (www.averyflynn.com) follow her on Twitter (@AveryFlynn) and Pinterest (pinterest.com/AveryFlynnBooks), and like her on her Facebook page (facebook.com/AveryFlynnAuthor). Also, if you figure out how to send Oreos through the Internet, she'll be your best friend for life. Contact her at avery@averyflynn.com. She'd love to hear from you!

Discover more category romance titles from Entangled Indulgence…

MILLIONAIRE UNDER THE MISTLETOE
a novel by Stefanie London

Stella Jackson would rather stab herself in the eye with her own stiletto than return to England. But to fulfill her grandfather's last wish, she has to spend Christmas at the estate she inherited from him…with the one man she wishes she could forget. Self-made millionaire Evan Foss wants one thing from Stella—her estate. But seeing her now, sexy and all grown up, tempts Evan to finish what started years ago between them.

RIGHT BILLIONAIRE, WRONG WEDDING
a *Sexy Billionaires* novel by Victoria Davies

Darian King has never met a challenge he couldn't handle–except planning his sister's wedding. His able assistant, Allison Reed, agrees to help, but what he doesn't expect is the spark that ignites between them. But he doesn't know her secret, and she fears that by the time the vows are exchanged, she won't just be leaving her job behind but her heart as well.

SOUTHERN NIGHTS AND SECRETS
a *Boys are Back in Town* novel by Robin Covington

Being a doctor is everything to me, but I'm not going to let bureaucrats tell me how to practice medicine. It's about saving lives no matter what, screw them and their paperwork. When the one woman I could never forget, Ginger Crawford, shows up as my boss all bets are off. The heat between us is tough to ignore but I have to if I want a future at this hospital. It isn't easy. Every time we argue, I want her even more. But I've got secrets she can never know, and she's always going to be way too good for me. So it's best if she hates me…at least that's what I keep telling myself.

Made in the USA
Columbia, SC
15 May 2018